GHOST STORIES
OF THE
DELAWARE COAST

David J. Seibold   Charles J. Adams III

EXETER HOUSE BOOKS
1990

GHOST STORIES
OF THE DELAWARE COAST

COPYRIGHT 1990

For information write:
EXETER HOUSE BOOKS
P.O. Box 91
11 West 8th St.
Barnegat Light, NJ 08006

ISBN: 0-9610008-9-9

PRINTED IN THE UNITED STATES OF AMERICA

TABLE OF CONTENTS

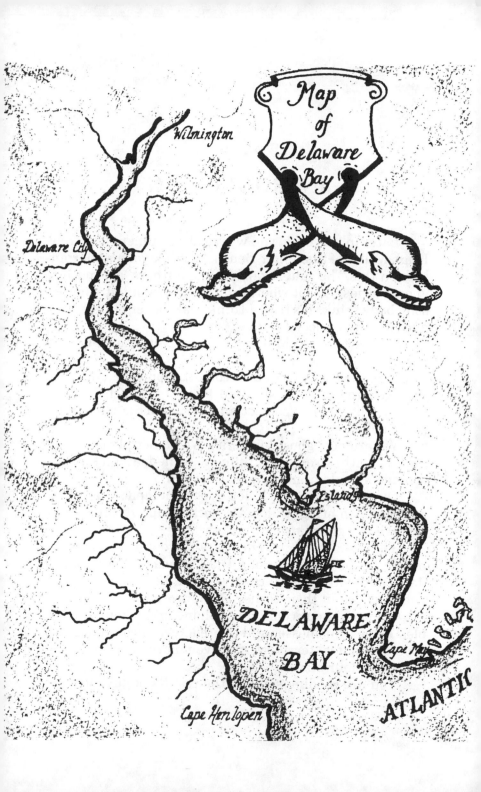

INTRODUCTION

Later in this book, you will read a comment from Rev. Hugh Miller of Slaughter Beach. "I think your whole outlook on this," he said regarding the authors' approach to ghost stories, "is not whether it's true or not but whether somebody thinks it's true. I think that's a very interesting and healthy outlook."

Thank you, Rev. Miller, and thank you, the reader, for picking up this book.

Rev. Miller is kind, and correct. Someone once said that you really don't want to know too much about a legend. That, too, is correct and very much a part of our philosophy.

We are not "ghost hunters." We do not ply the countryside with strange equipment aimed at picking up strange signals from the great beyond.

Our equipment includes a pen, notepad and, if we remember to bring it along, a pocket tape recorder.

We are ghost **story** hunters.

They're out there. They're all around. While some people in the villages along the Delaware Coast told us flatly and with finality that we would find no ghosts or ghost stories in their corner of the world, we persisted.

We spent hours on the telephone, more hours in peoples' homes, businesses and in predetermined rendezvous spots on neutral territory, and even more hours in libraries across four states.

You are reading some of the results of our quest.

What you are about to read reflects a bit of the history of the Delaware coastal regions, but this book does not pretend to masquerade as a history book.

It is nothing more than a collection of tales from the darker side of life along the sunny shore of the Diamond State.

These legends, these superstitions and these ghost stories indeed intertwine among the historical chronicles of the area. Dates and places, names and faces seem less important in this realm of our lives.

Delaware is an enchanted little state. Vague and sometimes closely guarded stories of headless spirits roaming the night, mysterious sects, voodoo, Indian rituals, pirates and ghosts of both the crowned and the commoner, the meek, murdered and murderer can be ferreted out of every corner from Newark to Fenwick Island.

In the pages that follow we will explore the ghosts and unexplained phenomena of the area along the Delaware coastline, and inland a reasonable number of miles. But to set the stage for this journey, let us briefly examine some of the more durable and popular folk tales and ghost stories that have come up in the annals of the state's proud and colorful history.

Perhaps no other city or town in Delaware is as "blessed" with ghostly goings-on than its bustling, charming capital of Dover.

Approaching the mini-metropolis from its major highway access routes, it is difficult to imagine any locales which would support the traditional aura needed for a ghostly setting. Even the darkest and stormiest night, it would seem at first glance, would be illuminated by a sign from a fast food restaurant or shopping center.

But it is deep within the capital district and just beyond where the ghosts of Dover wander on brick sidewalks and under the craggy limbs of ancient trees.

The legends are legion. It is said that a ghost stalks the 1790-era Hall Mansion on King Street. A lingering story places the headless ghost of infamous Patty Cannon (we shall hear more about her in the coming text) can be felt inside the Dover Public Library. Her skull, they say, is in repose in the library and her confused torso is in eternal search for its disembodied head.

The best known ghost of the Dover business district is the spectre of Samuel Chew, which may still haunt the Green.

Despite the fact that Chew rose to become a Delaware Supreme Court Chief Justice, he was the victim of banal ridicule for no other reason than his surname.

"Ahh-CHEW!" The mocking sound would be heard behind the jurist's back as he ambled around the town of Dover from his red-brick house on the Green to and from shops, offices and the court. Some hecklers would jawbone and chomp their jowls in a chewing motion, all to raise the hackles under the white-wig of the refined and respected judge.

The judge was buried in 1844, but the mockery of his name continued up to and during his funeral services, it is said.

Almost immediately following Samuel Chew's death and interment, rumors of his ghost returning ran rampant through Dover.

Described as a misty but clear figure of a man dressed in a black shroud or judge's robe and a white wig, the spirit was first noticed rising between the tombstones in the church graveyard in which Chew was buried.

The restless wraith apparently found its way across Dover, tormenting those who had teased and berated him in life, and scaring the bejeebers out of them by blowing out their lanterns at night and making tree branches sway on calm nights.

The steely-faced ghost would stare at those he chose to haunt and after a while the good people of Dover were so caught up in the reports of the ghostly judge that streets and roads were devoid of people after dark and the local tavern business plummeted.

At pubs such as the Inn of King George III and Cook's

Tavern, the proprietors pondered ways to exorcise the pesky spook and make Dover a safe place for mortals once again.

Following an accepted British tradition that would put to rest those souls which were not resting in peace, a hardy band of volunteers assembled at Cook's, hastened in the cover of night to the grave of Judge Chew and carried out yet another formal funeral service.

It is generally regarded that the second "burial" sent the spirit to its appointed courtroom in the sky, as the ghost was never seen again in 19th century Dover.

This is not necessarily so, however, for over the years since the "exorcism," a mysterious cloaked figure has indeed been spotted darting about the side streets and sidewalks of the Dover Green.

Should you encounter this entity, it would not be wise to tempt fate by faking a sneeze or a chewing motion!

Another ghostly vision has been reported along a stretch of Loockerman Street in Dover. It is the site of the grisly murder of a man named Couch Turn by Isaac West. It was reported that West brutally beat Turn with a hammer, stripped the skin from his victim, set fire to the second floor of the now-demolished Kirbin Building, and fled the scene.

West was brought to trial and acquitted for the crime, but the ghost of Couch Turn now paces eternally along Loockerman Street.

Rev. George A. Burslem, who told and re-told ghost stories from the darker side of Delaware, went as far as to predict that the best time to spot the ghost of Couch Turn — the SKINLESS ghost of Couch Turn, we might add — is on December 4, the anniversary date of the 1872 crime.

Elsewhere in Dover, a ghostly witch supposedly prowls the Green, and the pathetic spirit of a young girl has been seen walking in the misty moonlight along Water Street.

By far the most noteworthy of all the Kent County ghosts, and quite possibly of all the ghost stories of Delaware, haunt a home no less imposing than Woodburn, the official residence of the governor of Delaware.

Tales are told of secret doors, a secret tunnel and as many as five ghosts who float through the hallowed halls of the dignified three-story Federal building at 151 Kings Highway.

Framed by manicured shrubs, myrtle and tall pines, Woodburn is supposedly haunted by spirits which range from a mysterious young girl to a malevolent slavenapper.

The respected judge George P. Fisher is the source of the story of an encounter with one of the kindlier spirits of Woodburn in the early 1800s.

The itinerant Methodist preacher Lorenzo Dow was invited by the residents of Woodburn, a Dr. and Mrs. M. W. Bates, to share a night's rest and breakfast at their home.

Early in the morning, Rev. Dow left his bed chamber on the second floor and descended the main staircase toward the dining room and breakfast.

On the landing, a gentlemen with knee breeches, a powdered wig and a ruffled shirt approached the minister. Not a word was exchanged, but the two men exchanged bows and continued on their respective courses up and down the stairs.

At the breakfast table, the Bates' felt honored to ask Rev. Dow to offer grace. He agreed to, but deferred to the gentleman he had just greeted on the stairs, noting that it might be proper if they wait for the other guest to join them at the table.

Mrs. Bates informed Rev. Dow kindly that there was no other guests in the house.

Then who did Rev. Lorenzo Dow meet on the steps that morning?

While she hastily changed the subject after informing Dow that they were alone in the house at the time, Mrs. Dow later confided to him that the man he encountered may well have been her father. Dow's description of his dress and manner seemed to fit that of her father, who had died in Woodburn and at that time had been in his grave for ten years!

That same spirit, or at least one with the same basic mode of fashion, has been seen wandering the staircase, halls and rooms of Woodburn on several other occasions. To some, he has become known as "the colonel."

There is a general feeling among those who believe and respect the story that the ghost is an officer from the Revolutionary War era who spent time at Woodburn after it was built in 1790.

Whatever, this same kindly spirit has been suspected as the unseen entity that has emptied wine glasses (and sometimes even bottles) in the dark of night. Dr. Frank Hall, who was the last private owner of Woodburn before it became the official governor's residence in 1966, reported unexplained activities in the place, and at least three employees of the mansion in recent years have sworn to have seen the colonel striding gently and ghostly in the corridors of Woodburn.

The other ghostly residents of the mansion include the little girl, described as wearing a red gingham dress and seen often in the garden, and a chain-dragging, moaning, miserable spirit who has made himself known on several occasions both inside and outside the house.

The little girl reportedly came out to play at the inauguration party of Gov. Michael Castle in 1985. Several women felt the very distinct tugging at their dresses from what they described as an invisible child.

That same year, three young girls and their teacher received permission to spend a night in the mansion in an attempt to witness, and even video tape the perambulations of the ghost.

While nothing conclusive came of it, the girls did report some unusual problems with the video camera and claimed that a suitcase stand leaning against an upstairs bed flipped open on its own as they passed by it.

The more audible spirit is believed to be one of the raiders who pounced on Woodburn during its time as a "station" along the Underground Railroad.

The ill-fated slavenapper attempted to flee after finding resistance, but somehow found himself hanged by the neck on a poplar tree near the house. His dying gasps and moans, as well as the rattling of the leg irons and chains he was carrying to carry out his trade, can be heard to this day on the property.

Still another tale of the unknown at Woodburn was told by Judge Fisher, who lived in the house in the mid-19th century.

A friend had come to spend the night with the judge, and that friend was given the elegant former bedroom of Charles Hillyard, the first occupant and owner of Woodburn nearly a century before.

As Fisher's guest prepared to bed down for the night, he looked up into a corner of the bedroom and in the dim light of one candle saw the faint but very plain image of an old man, sitting near the hearth.

So startling was the vision that the man fainted and fell to the floor. The sound of his fall drew Fisher to rush to the room, where the friend explained his experience.

There are many, many more intriguing and chilling tales of ghosts around Delaware, and more will follow in this volume. But this is, as the title suggests, a book on the ghosts of the Delaware Coast, so will you please come with us now to the shores of the bay and ocean and explore a netherworld where many fear to tread?

We're glad you chose to come along. You're good company.

THE SMOKY FACE

Gregory King had no idea what was to happen that day when he and a friend set out for a visit to another buddy's house along a quiet street in the tiny backwater development known as Bay Vista on Rehoboth Bay.

King was visibly shaken as he recalled the memories that had been buried deep within his mind for more than ten years. Over the handsome bar of Gilligan's Bar and Grille in Lewes, where he was employed at the time of the interview, he remembered the encounter he had that day with the unknown.

"Our friend wasn't home at the time," he said. "We knew that, and I can't really remember exactly why we went there."

He paused often, smiling a nervous smile and fighting the shudders that swept his soul as he related his tale.

"The two of us walked around the house to the backyard and to the garage. Out of the corner of my eye, I saw something in a garage window."

King described what he saw as a "smoky face," barely discernible but positively identifiable as a human face, or at least he had hoped so.

But then, something very disconcerting happened.

"That face began to slowly move across the window horizontally," King said, drawing a deep breath. It wavered from side to side as he watched intently and with mounting fear and trepidation.

He felt that it might have had a logical explanation. Perhaps it was simply someone inside the garage, peering out at the pair of petrified pals through a cloudy window pane. That proposition was dashed quickly, however, when the mysterious face suddenly rose and appeared in the second highest frame of the window.

It was then that King and his companion realized that something was very wrong.

"The face had no body attached to it," King said as the mask of his bravado vanished. "I could see quite clearly that there was positively no body there."

In the fleeting moments of the experience, the two young men grew increasingly anxious. The detached head, with its blank face, floated to and fro across the windows and then up and then down.

To this day, Greg King swears to the veracity of the episode, and remains befuddled over the presence in the window. "Maybe it was some sort of guardian angel, or something," he offered hesitatingly. "But whatever it was, it was scary and we got out of there as soon as we could."

Their departure on that memorable evening was so quick, King added, that his compatriate broke an ankle in the hasty getaway.

A similar incident still brings fearful thoughts to a pair of Georgetown girls who faced the unknown while cruising on a family houseboat on Indian River Bay.

"We were somewhere near Holts Landing, I believe," recalled Pam, who asked that her real name not be used for fear of ridicule. It was really early in the morning, and it was kind of misty and foggy. The sun was just coming up and it hadn't yet burned off the clouds."

"There's really not much to tell," she continued, "and I have only told a few people because I'm afraid they'll make a fool of me. Heck, maybe you will, too. But I know that I saw what I saw that day, and nobody can change my mind."

A perky teenager with strawberry blonde hair and a gift of gab, Pam recalled that as she and her friend (who also wishes to remain anonymous) chugged their way past a spit of land on the southern shore of Indian River Bay, they were distracted by an eerie, moaning sound.

"This is where everybody I have told starts to go off on me," Pam said. "But there it was, off in the distance, a low, sort of growling sound. Now, unusual sounds out there early in the morning aren't really unusual, but this one was. It could have been the motor of a boat or even a car, I thought at first. As I listened closer, and it seemed to get a little louder, though, I felt that it was from an animal or maybe even a human.

"Whatever, my friend and I heard it for a good three minutes. It wasn't really growling, but it was more like a sad moaning sound, like something or someone was in pain."

Pam shook her head and assured the interviewer that there was more . . . much more.

"I tried to pin down the spot from where the sound was coming, and as I scanned the shore, everything was real quiet and empty. But then, I almost died!

"Right at the edge of the water, sort of half on land and half on the water, I saw a dull glow. It was a shaft of milky light at first, vertical and with no real shape. I guess you're starting to think I'm crazy by now."

No, Pam, not at all.

"Well, my friend was not looking at that direction at the time, and I was too spellbound to call for her. I just stood there, trying to figure out what the heck I was watching. Well, all of a sudden, this form started to get thinner and, as God is my witness, started to take the shape of a human. It really did.

"Then, I thought for sure I would croak when I felt this hand on my shoulder. I don't think I screamed, but I know I jumped enough to rock the pontoon boat. I turned around quickly and it was my friend's hand!"

Pam said she and her friend spoke not a word. As it turned out, her friend had also seen the vision rising from the water and slowly taking the shape of a person.

"We stood there like two crazy people watching as this, this thing just seemed to bob on the water, just a couple feet from the shore, and kept looking more and

3

more like it was going to develop into a human being. It was freaky. Real freaky.

"I guess I better add somewhere along the way that my friend and I don't drink, we don't do drugs and we are basically normal people who never gave any thoughts at all to the possibility that ghosts exist. I'm not even saying this was a ghost. Who knows what it was.

"We must have watched the figure for a good minute, although it seemed like a couple of hours. There was no doubt that the moaning sound was coming from the same area, and we naturally figured that it was coming from the form we were watching."

It wasn't until a few days after the incident on Indian River Bay that Pam and her girlfriend sorted things out and came up with a theory that may have a basis in truth.

"Anyway, we watched this and listened to it, and although it never really became anything recognizable, there was no doubt in either of our minds that it was there, and it was making a sound, and it was more than likely a ghost.

"When it was all over, the form seemed to evaporate, and really, and I know this really sounds like a doozy, just seep back into the water.

"After we calmed down a little, and took the boat very quickly to the other side of the bay, we got to thinking about what we saw. We thought that maybe, if this thing was a ghost, it might have been the ghost of an Indian. After all, it is Indian River, and I was always taught that Indians lived down that way. So maybe it was the lost soul of an Indian who was just trying to get attention or find the happy hunting ground."

The two sensible, intelligent young women do not make light of their experience, or their proposition. "If that is the case, that ghosts really do exist and what we saw and heard was the spirit of an Indian, then it is sad to know that this one never found its heaven or whatever. I wish I knew more about this kind of thing and wish there was something I could do to put the spirit to rest."

THE GHOST OF FIDDLER'S HILL AND OTHER STORIES

We met her on a Sunday morning between church and one of her civic commitments later that day. It had been a game of tag up to that point, but we were told that if anyone in Sussex County would know anything about its ghost stories and history, it would be Hazel Brittingham.

Elegant and vivacious, the writer, historian and community leader was gracious as we settled into our seats at a window table at the Rose and Crown in Lewes.

"Ghosts, eh?" Mrs. Brittingham barely took a breath before opening up a bag stuffed with papers and books. Always on a hectic schedule, she is also always willing to sandwich in time for anyone who shares her passion for the heritage of Sussex County.

Over coffee and tea, we chatted.

"That's right, Mrs. Brittingham, ghosts," we replied.

She was quick to establish that the notion of ghosts and phantoms isn't exactly pervasive in the history and lore of lower Delaware. "I have next to nothing on them," she said, "but I'll tell you what — I think a house with a ghost is much more valuable than a house without one."

The historian she is, Mrs. Brittingham was talking of an intrinsic, not monetary value that a ghost story adds to a property.

"A house with a legend is very important to me," she continued. "There's more to mystery than there is to fact, and I like that."

She rattled off remembrances of many of the fine old

sea captains' and traders' homes that still line the streets of Lewes, and spoke of the richness and singular characteristics of each.

She recalled the massacres, the marauders and the magic of Cape Henlopen and its long history and conjured up thoughts of mystery and history.

Pirates and treasure, superstitions and traditions, the thoughts rolled from her mind.

Indeed, there was one solid ghost story that rose to the surface of her memory. It was the Ghost of Fiddler's Hill.

This particular tale is one which has been so warped and disfigured by time and re-telling that it has lost virtually all of whatever credibility it might ever have had. Still, its basic framework is a bit chilling.

If you approach Fiddler's Hill on a quiet night, under a new moon or thick layer of clouds, you may meet up with the phantom fiddler.

You may hear the faint fiddling music first, or the misty figure of the fiddler may appear in the dark. Either way, they say, your visit to Fiddler's Hill will be a memorable one.

Fiddler's Hill is really a knoll at Rabbit's Ferry, along Road 277 just a short ride southwest of Lewes. It is fairly easy to visualize a time when modern homes did not dot the roadside, when it was a gravel land that crossed over Love Creek near Goslee Mill Pond and when gypsies are said to have congregated down at what some called the "dirt hole."

Today, the scene has changed. When the legend first took root there, it must have been a far more mysterious place.

The legend has it that two young men were courting a particular lass who lived on the hill. One of them decided to scare off the other when he came to visit the woman. He figured that if he hid in a tree and fiddled wildly as the rival approached on horse (or oxen) and wagon, the sound would scare him away.

Sure enough, as the man rounded the turn and began to climb the hill toward the woman's home, the fiddler employed his skills.

The animals bolted. The suitor was scared away. But in his enthusiasm, the fiddler tumbled from the tree limb, dropped to the ground and died of a broken neck.

It is the spirit and his ghostly fiddling which haunts Fiddler's Hill and gives it its name.

Hazel Brittingham arches her eyebrows and serves up a smirk at this notion. She does not, however, totally refute the story.

Kind enough to lead us to the haunted hill, Mrs. Brittingham as well took time to relate an extension of the legend and how some Lewes locals had their wits scared out of them one night a few years back.

"They went out one night," she said of two daring and devilish local boys, "and one went up into a tree with a fiddle. The other hid in the trees with a sheet or something. As passersby came along, they reenacted the legend.

"They did it one night and then another, and by the third night, as word spread about the 'ghosts' out on Fiddler's Hill, practically all the school kids of Sussex County went out there.

"The home ec teacher from Lewes went," she continued with a building chuckle in her voice, "and she fainted dead away. As I recall, Dr. James Beebe Jr. was there, and almost everybody in town eventually showed up!"

Among the historic homes of Lewes, the Lubker House, which was originally located on W. 2nd Street but was later moved to Pilottown Road, is among the most storied.

It was in that house that a deep reddish-brown stain was permanently imbedded in the floorboards of an upstairs bedroom.

The stain, legend has it, is blood. The blood is from an early Lewes settler who was murdered by pirates. His blood, and his spirit, remains as a very part of the old home.

For another ghost story, in another historic and very familiar Lewes building, we turned to another very familiar name in local historical circles.

The story of the possible haunting of the Cannonball House is next.

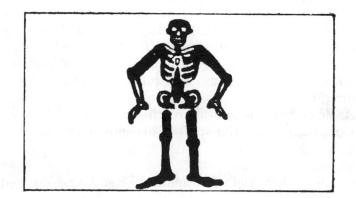

THE GHOST OF THE CANNONBALL HOUSE

Henry Marshall is one of the keepers of the historical flame of Lewes. Retired from the U.S. Postal Service since 1971, the energetic man has been instrumental in the continued preservation and promotion of the Cannonball House as an historical property.

He talked freely in his spacious Lewes home. He talked of his goals of establishing a formal historical museum in the Cannonball House, talked of the architectural challenges presented by the layout and age of the Front Street building, and talked of his colorful and meaningful life.

As he talked, the audible reminders of one of Henry's other passions broke the spell of his conversation.

Bells.

Chimes.

Clocks. They ticked, clicked, dinged and donged almost incessantly.

"Oh, pay no mind to them," he laughed.

As the bells sounded, the topic turned to the Cannonball House and the very real possibility that a ghost walks among its tender timbers.

Of any building in Lewes, the Cannonball House is a treasure that vividly depicts a relic of the town's past. A portion of the structure dates to 1743, according to Marshall, but is quick to establish that the basic building, the "new part," as he calls it, was built sometime around 1790.

Now surrounded by a yard graced by the work of the Sussex Gardeners and outfitted with numerous nautical artifacts, the one-time home of David Rowland is a splendid example of cypress-shingled architecture typical of the early years of Lewes.

Imbedded in a wall for effect is a cannonball — the stark reminder of April 6, 1813, when the building was hit by a cannonball as a British frigate pounded the town during the War of 1812.

"It was in the oldest part of the building," Marshall contends, "where the fireplace is, where the original owners lived. They slept up in the loft at the start, and later on they added the other part.

"There's a stairway that goes up to that loft, and there's a doorway that leads up to it." It is that doorway, he continued, which is the site of a mystery that has befuddled Marshall for years and has changed his entire outlook on the supernatural.

"That door was always left open, but it did have a latch lock on it," he said. "But no matter how often we locked it and latched it securely, the door would swing open. We never gave it any thought that it was anything but the breeze of gravity or whatever, but the door would always open up even after we had latched it."

Eventually, Marshall and another Cannonball House volunteer got the idea to hammer a firm nail over the latch after securing it so there would be no possible way it could open without extreme force.

"Once, we went to close it up for the winter, and we had to secure the latch with the nail to keep a little heat inside the room and make sure the door wouldn't open on its own again.

"We got it nailed — we drove the nail in about two inches — just over the latch. It was really tightly sealed, there was no doubt about it.

"Well, every once in a while over the winter months, we would go into the house to what I call 'stir up the air' so it wouldn't get a stale or damp feeling inside.

"One time, though, we came back," he continued, slowing the pace of his conversation so we would understand clearly what he was implying, "and that door, the door we nailed shut, was wide open."

Nothing else in the house was disturbed, he assured his interviewers, and there was no appearance whatsoever of foul play.

"I said to the other man 'don't move!' I'm gonna get down on my hands and knees, I told him, and look for that nail. It wasn't in the door, above the latch where we put it, and I couldn't find it anywhere on the bare floor."

Only Marshall and his associate had keys to the Cannonball House at the time, so they knew someone else did not come in and disturb the doorway.

"That nail was gone. The door was wide open, and, well . . .," Marshall measured the words he thought he would never utter, ". . . I believe it just might have been the work of . . . a ghost!"

As he shook his head, perhaps questioning his own assertion, he detailed what little is known about the life and times inside the old dwelling. He talked of the time a family lived there and a tragedy struck.

"There was a fireplace in the old part, and at one time, something flared out and one of the residents was burned to death," he recalled. He would not go as far as venturing that the victim has taken on a ghostly presence in the Cannonball House, but he is at a loss to explain his personal touch with the unknown and unexplainable.

He is not, and never has been, a firm believer in ghosts, but he cannot deny the mysterious events of the Cannonball House and their possibly ghostly implications.

As he searched his mind for other ghost stories in and around Lewes, all he could remember is a vague story about another door which would open on its own volition in a house on West Second Street, much to the amazement and shock of an old friend.

"I never really thought too much about ghosts at all," he said. "Or at least I didn't before what happened to us at the Cannonball House that day. After that, though, I knew that something was very strange."

"CHARLIE," THE POLTERGEIST OF SHIPCARPENTER SQUARE

Ghosts sometimes have the misfortune of receiving whimsical names from confused mortals who are even more confused by the unexplainable occurrences in their lives which are attributed to spooks.

In the case of a cantankerous spirit at a home on Third Street's Shipcarpenter Square, the ghost was called Charlie.

The story was related to the authors by writer/editor Barbara Gallas via Joan Nagy, who has had her own brushes with the unknown.

Jack Vessels, Joan's brother-in-law, was working on the restoration project in the late 1970s when the incident took place.

Thought to have been owned originally by a sea captain, the 19th century shingled house had all the earmarks of a possible ghostly connection.

A ship's stone ballast became the foundation for the home, and its heavy timbers were once timbers of a deck. The place was ripe for haunting, if some researchers and theorists are to be believed.

The presence of these ancient materials could, as some more scholarly investigators purport, make such a structure a veritable magnet for ghosts.

The authors have researched hundreds of reports of hauntings throughout the world, and if there is any pattern at all which can be determined, it is not geographic or socio-economic or demographic, but architectural.

Be it an old farmhouse on a high, windy Pennsylvania mountain, a ragged bungalow in the Pine Barrens of New Jersey or a castle in the Bavarian Alps, nearly every "haunted house" which offered a story that is anywhere remotely believable shared one trait: Something had been done to alter the place and change its original design. It would be too easy to surmise, then, that this process of modification or alteration simply confused whatever ghost might have lurked inside and "released" it for all (or some) to see (or hear, or sense). That, alas, would be too simple.

Perhaps a slightly more complex, and at once fantastic yet feasible explanation could be that when an architectural feature of a building — new or old; city, town or country — is tampered with, the actual force field or dimension in which the "ghost" is imprisoned is indeed changed to the point where there may be a scientific reason to consider the possibility that ghosts, or at least a form of energy we call "ghosts" (it would be a hard sell, a book entitled "Energy Stories of the Delaware Coast") really do exist.

It may be worth noting that the capacity of the human mind seems to be ever expanding, and virtually limitless. Its capacity to understand itself travels over new horizons of comprehension almost constantly. What was unheard of psychologically and psychically just decades ago is now commonly accepted. Technology, the mechanical manifestation of the mind, has aided in this acceptance.

The authors' favorite and daringly rational explanation of ghostly occurrences is really quite simple, but does require some tolerance and thought.

Technology has enabled man to record his voice and almost every sound around him on rust — ferrous oxide — the refined product we call recording tape.

Through electrical impulses, these sounds are recorded permanently on rust. Imagine now, the electrical impulses of the human brain at the time of extreme trauma, such as a sudden death. Could not these electrical impulses, these "brain waves," which normally travel through the complex human nervous system be burst from the confines of the body and into the atmosphere around it? Could not these impulses in turn be recorded much as on tape on any waiting piece of ferrous oxide nearby?

As an example, an old house, and especially a remodeled or altered old house, could harbor inside it "ghosts" of all ilk simply through a phenomenon of nature.

This is not to suggest that spirits may simply dwell in another dimension within the walls and under floorboards of an old building. But what about the simple implements that help keep the walls and floorboards together?

Nails. Rusty nails.

Again, could it not be possible that these electrical impulses emitted by the brain at a cataclysmic time could be "recorded" on the rust and "played back" at a later time? Could it not be possible that the receptive mind such as that of a "medium" could receive these impulses? Could they not then be played back through the medium as a vivid account of the innermost secrets of the life and death of the victim?

These are bold propositions, perhaps, but a century ago, the idea of tape recording was in itself preposterous.

As this book is not a detailed history book of the Delaware Coast, nor is it a treatise on the scientific evidence for or against the possibility that ghosts exist. Therefore, let us head back toward Shipcarpenter's Square for the story.

This noisy, ne'er-do-well ghost, this "Charlie," is reported to have pestered a team of contractors working at the Third Street home. Stacks of wood tumbled, a pile of bricks shook, and a mysterious, free-standing letter "C" appeared in the middle of a freshly-trowelled patch of concrete.

But the most telling of the stories to come from that restoration project was from one worker who claimed that as he was adding new shingles to one portion of the house, a cloaked, dark figure passed close by him.

Startled, he angled to find the source or identity of this obvious illusion. He failed to do so. Time after time, in spot after spot throughout the house, the shadowy figure appeared once again.

He decided to write off the figure as a trick of the lighting or, quite simply, a shadow. Although there appeared to be nothing capable of casting such a shadow, it was, in the name of reason, only a shadow.

Or was it?

THE GHOST OF THE ADDY-SEA

Down Bethany Beach way, the general perception is that the handsome little town is a relatively quiet yet hospitable family getaway where days are sun-drenched and evenings are breezy and relaxed.

A nice place, this Bethany Beach. Not the kind of place which would be the home of one of the most haunted of all houses in Delaware, now is it?

Yes, it is!

At Oceanview and the beach, near the boxy beach houses and overlooking the fun-in-the-sun crowd that romps on the sandy strand just over the dunes, is one of the most endearing bed and breakfast operations of the Delaware Coast. It is also a hostelry for some rather insistent yet benevolent spirits who walk its ancient floors and dart about its inviting rooms.

The wind from the ocean rushes through delicate fingers of gingerbread that fan out at the top of the columns along the broad front porch of the Addy-Sea. Dune grass and rushes whoosh gently, and protective snow fences creak and whine.

If the trappings of the twentieth century that abut the Addy-Sea can be stripped away from the setting, it is clear why the ghosts find the old building so inviting.

Shutters frame windows that bear the weatherbeaten scars of many a storm. Cedar shingles extend above the supportive columns and on the sloping hip roof. The building itself tells many tales.

But the tales of the Addy-Sea are not of architectural splendor, they are of ghosts.

On the streetside porch, a keystone of pebbles sets the stage for the story.

Within the jagged frame are names — John M. & Jennie M. Addy, Will-Charlie-Walter-Ann — the family which gave the place its name and, perhaps, at least one of its ethereal residents.

Frances Gravatte knows all about the ghosts of the Addy-Sea. And, she'd be willing to put down her chores and talk to anyone interested enough in the tales. That's exactly what happened one autumn afternoon when a pair of coastal ghost hunters dropped by.

"Oh, yes," Frances said without wincing, "we certainly have ghosts in here." The owner of the 90-year old, eleven-room bed and breakfast says there are no televisions in the rooms (too noisy and distracting) and no air conditioners (the sea breezes are more than enough for cooling), but there are plenty of ghosts.

It seems that John Addy was a plumber from Pittsburgh who built the Addy-Sea as a new home in 1904. His family became one of the first to settle in then-remote Bethany Beach.

Addy may not have counted on the ravages of the storms when he positioned his home. Repeatedly in 1920 and 1924, severe storms battered the Addy-Sea until its owner was obliged to hire teams of mules and "darkies" to move the structure from its original site. It was moved a second time to escape further threats from storms and erosion.

These transplants account for the fact that some of the joints don't quite join, some of the angles aren't exactly right, and some of the doorways and floors sag a bit. In all, these little misfortunes are nothing more than idiosyncracies of a most magnificent old building.

When you enter the Addy-Sea, you enter a splendid museum of Victoriana. A sturdy marble fireplace greets you, and as your fingers walk through the guest register you notice names from as far away as San Francisco have called the Addy-Sea home for a night or two. "Loved the dolphins . . .," ". . . very relaxing . . .," the comments read.

Every inch of the Addy-Sea is carefully and lovingly tended. The guest rooms are massive yet comfortable. Cooling breezes waft over wood and brass beds and broad windows provide sweeping seascapes.

Yes, some doorways are uneven, doors are shaved so they may close. In a way, the elegance of the Addy-Sea is a faded elegance. But she is in no way a has-been starlet waiting by the telephone.

Frances and Leroy Gravatte were long acquainted with the charms of the Addy-Sea. It had been a tourist home since 1935, and after spending summers in a home across the street, Gravatte purchased the Addy-Sea in 1974.

So who are the ghosts of the old home? It has been said that one is that of Kurtz Addy, who Frances Gravatte describes as a "rowdy" member of the old family.

She says Kurtz is known to have fallen from the roof of the building, and it is his phantom footsteps which can be heard clomping on that roof when all conditions are right.

Frances disputes, or at least doubts, that the footsteps which have been heard by several people are those of the late Kurtz Addy.

She would prefer to believe that they belong to one Paul Dulaney, a well-known swimmer and handyman who did work for the Addy family during the glory years of the property.

It is Dulaney's ghost, says Mrs. Gravatte, which has been heard and even seen on the third floor.

Unlike the story attached to the unfortunate Kurtz Addy, Dulaney was not a victim of a fall from the roof. Frances says he did do shingle work on the roof and siding, but after all that high construction work, he met his death after falling from a peach tree in Georgia.

"Oh, yes, we've seen his ghost up there, we really

have," says Frances. "We've seen a figure in the bed. My granddaughter felt a cold hand touch her up there."

That granddaugher, in her late 20s at the time, has been among the many who have also reported hearing mysterious organ music echoing through the corridors and rooms of the house, and disembodied conversation emanating from empty rooms.

While she dismisses the lofty footsteps as those of Kurtz Addy, Frances Gravatte does not discharge Mr. Addy as a prime suspect for the haunting of other sections of the building.

She speaks of a time when a still unexplained incident took place in Room One of the inn. "I walked in the room," she says, "and in the middle of the floor was a piece of brown-stained old newspaper.

"I picked it up, looked at it, and it was the newspaper obituary of Kurtz Addy!"

How it got there, Frances does not know. She does know, however, that it never appeared anywhere before that time.

"One night," she continues, "I was sleeping there in Room One. At about four o'clock in the morning, an imitation oil lamp just fell on my face."

There have been several unexplained and eerie events over the years at the Addy-Sea. Neighbors and guests alike have reported strange sights, sounds and sensations in various parts of the building.

Mrs. Gravatte has caught the whiff of alien perfume wafting through the upstairs rooms. She surmises it is the unearthly aroma of a long-gone guest or Addy family member.

One of the most disconcerting feelings to have been experienced at the Addy-Sea is the pronounced shaking which has been felt by certain people as they bathed in a fine copper bath tub in the bathroom of Room One. It was Mr. Addy's room, and the plumber had that particular tub brought down to Bethany Beach from his Pittsburgh home.

Some of the events which have taken place at the inn simply defy any rational explanation. They may not be of a ghostly nature, but then again, who can be certain? "One thing that happened was very odd," says Mrs. Gravatte. "We had just bought the place and our busboy was out swimming. I was in the closet downstairs cleaning hymnals out of it. The closet door slowly creaked shut behind me. Finally, the busboy came back and heard me banging from inside. He came to my rescue and asked me who locked me in there. I couldn't say, of course. But I think it might have been Kurtz!"

In addition to the lovely Room One, at least two other guest rooms have been graced with ghostly goings-on. "My in-laws would like to sit up in Room Six and listen to the organ play, and it really did," says Mrs. Gravatte. "I think the presence some have felt in Room Eleven is that of Paul Dulaney," she adds.

The Addy-Sea has had a long and colorful existence there by the beach. It has survived fierce storms, a couple of relocations, a stint as an ammunition storage site during the war, and now the noble role of a bed and breakfast.

Sure, sweet organ music comes from the thin air. A bath tub shimmies, footsteps are heard in the night and the answering machine of the telephone will click itself on occasionally (as it did during our interview with Frances Gravatte).

Do these incidents frighten the Gravattes, or their guests? "Oh, no," says Frances, "every one of our ghosts are very tame and friendly. They just want all of us to know they're here."

THINGS THAT GO SLOSH
IN THE NIGHT

Between the towns of Selbyville and Gumboro, just north of the Delaware-Maryland line, lies one of the most mysterious stretches of land in all of Delaware.

It is actually a mushy mix of land and bog, a dark and foreboding area with a colorful history — the Great Cypress Swamp.

Most locals call it "Burnt Swamp," and it seems that most locals don't really know why they call it that.

"Ah baleeve it's cuz it cawt awn farr wun tamm," said one man from Selbyville in a distinctive Delmarva drawl.

Yes, the swamp "cawt on farr" more than once. The very composition of the swamp, and despite its moist surface, makes it flammable and vulnerable to blazes which can spread into underground cypress tree trunks and peat.

The most popular explanation of how the swamp became known colloquially as "Burnt Swamp" stems from a fire in 1930.

Among the many enterprises carried out in the rich and remote reaches of the swamp was the illegal distillation of moonshine during Prohibition. In 1930, one of the stills exploded, touching off a conflagration that spread quickly throughout the sprawling fen which has been called the "Delaware Everglades."

The blaze blackened trees and underbrush, and another element of mystery was added to an already legendary region.

Geologically, the swamp is a surviving pool from the last ice age, when what is now Delaware was the ocean. The sea retreated, but the pocket of soggy remnants known as Burnt Swamp remained. In other terms, the swamp, once many times larger than its present size, became the headwaters of many streams and rivers. In still other terms, it was where native Americans and then escaped slaves found perilous but relatively safe refuge. Gum trees, cedars and cypress flourish in the depths of the swamp. The gum forests once provided the raw material that went into the manufacturing of baskets. The cypress stands were literally "mined" and their deep-seated peat was fashioned by hard-working laborers into weather-resistant shingles.

Since the mid-19th century, the swamp has been greatly shrunken in size by drainage ditches that added arable soil to its fringes.

One of the forgotten industries of the Burnt Swamp was the spearing and shooting of large bull frogs and turtles that dwelled in the ooze of the swamp. Enjoyed later by Philadelphia diners as turtle soup, the creatures were taken in great numbers by enterprising locals.

But there have been other denizens of the swamp which have been more elusive and far more threatening than frogs and turtles.

Cooperheads and water moccasins once thrived in the muck of Burnt Swamp, and there was a time when bear's roamed the loam deep within the bounds of the bog.

"Yeah, they said there was 'bars' in there," said Cordelia Daisey. Cordelia lives on the edge of the swamp, in a handsome home which was shingled by her grandfather in cypress taken from the dark, watery forest which looms just beyond her family farm fields.

She talked of the briars and huckleberries which alternately grated and gratified those who ventured into the swamp.

Modern, prosperous farms with fields of corn and soybean and houses of chickens now rim the ancient swamp. Traffic whizzes through the heart of it on Route 54. There is even an observation point along the route at which one may pull aside, take a short walk and peer into the thick of the swamp.

Mud squishes under the shoes, sticky spider webs descend from tree branches, and all around are the sounds of the birds and animals that dwell in the mire.

Frogs burp and leap, and the pungent, putrid smell of rancid, rotting vegetation is inescapable.

Even by day, the Burnt Swamp seemingly reeks with an aura of mystery. And that is today, only steps away from the causeway which traverses the swamp. One can only imagine the eerie atmosphere which must have prevailed a century or two ago, when the swamp was five or six times its present size and even more forbidding.

It is from that time that the lurid legends of the swamp were born, and some still linger in the minds and souls of those who live in southern Sussex County.

"On dark, cloudy days there may be heard from the depths of the swamp the sound of the 'old man' riving out his shingles, hour after hour, as he used to do. He is a ghost, too."

The words are from a Federal Writers' Project book published in 1938 by the Works Progress Administration (WPA). The memory of the moonshine still blast which sparked the year-long swamp fire was still fresh in the writers' minds, and although that fire put an end to the shingle-making, folks interviewed at the time could still recall the time when that industry thrived.

The authors' reference to the "ghost" of the old shingle maker was metaphoric, but much stronger stories of the unknown have sprung from the swamp over the years.

One of the regional historians who has recorded the swamp legends is Dorothy W. Pepper.

An accomplished author, she chatted in her Fenwick Island home about the most enduring of them, the elusive entity she referred to in one of her books as "the swamp creature."

The tale follows familiar motifs as it unfolds. It seems there was fair evidence that at one time a game warden gunned down some stray, wild dogs which were roaming in and around Burnt Swamp. He buried the carcasses within the bounds of the swamp, only to pass by the graves a few days later and notice they had been savagely attacked.

He found the remains of the dogs to be half-eaten by something obviously much larger and much more fierce than anything that had been seen in the swamp.

The first, rational thought was that it was a bear. Bears, as was noted, were frequently seen in the earlier years of the swamp's history, and the brutal treatment of the dogs' bodies had "bear" written all over it.

A search throughout the swamp, however, turned up no evidence that a bear was lurking within it.

A minor hysteria ensued. Sweeping through the minds (and perhaps the imaginations) of young and old alike were images of swamp monsters, hybrid man-beasts and horrible things that went slosh in the night.

Dorothy Pepper told of several folks from the Selbyville area who actually reported seeing a hairy creature wending its way through the swamp. It moaned and groaned, they said. It was a fearsome beast, they said.

This legend of the swamp "thing" persisted, and it is still in circulation today. But Mrs. Pepper was quick to offer one explanation for at least one variation of the creature story.

She remembered the time her parents bought a very expensive, extravagant raccoon coat for her when she was a student at the University of Delaware. It would, they knew, keep young Dorothy warm for many winters.

Indeed it did. But eventually, it became rather threadbare, and was in no real shape to continue to use as an outergarment.

Dorothy's nephew, Fred Stevens, spotted the old coat in a closet one day, and asked if he could borrow it as part of a Halloween getup. Dorothy consented.

Fred's idea was to wrap himself in the furry old coat, complete the costume with more fake hair and dark clothing, and hide out along the road that led through Burnt Swamp, scaring the pants off anyone who ventured by.

The clever, slightly mischievous prank took its toll of many an innocent passerby that October. And that, chuckled Dorothy Pepper, may have been the origin of the Legend of the Swamp Creature.

May have been.

THE GIRL OF THE DUNES

The sea does strange things to people.

The relentless roll of the surf and the seemingly endless bounds of the ocean can mesmerize, hypnotize and mystify the strongest of wills.

It is easy, then, to understand how stories of "phantom ships," mermaids and sea monsters can be generated by minds so boggled by the enormity of the sea.

And take note, please, placid and peaceful Cape Henlopen has all of these ethereal entities, and each will be addressed in later chapters.

Let us now, however, examine an equally baffling motif as related by a young couple who were forever changed by an experience on the dunes of the Delaware shore.

For fear that their story may fall into the hands of less enlightened friends and especially less tolerant employers, the authors accepted a trade of anonymity for story. We shall call them Gina and Jeff.

It can be told that both are on an upwardly mobile track in responsible positions in the Virginia officeburbs of Washington, D.C. Jeff works for a media and communications firm while Gina is employed in a government research facility. They are married, childless at the time of this writing, and graduates of the same prestigious university.

"From the very beginning," Jeff stated firmly in an interview in a summer home on Indian River Bay, "I must tell you that neither Gina nor I have never believed much in ghostly things, we didn't really enjoy those kinds of movies or books, and quite honestly I think we both thought anybody who got into such things as seances and that sort of thing were a little off center."

Gina concurred. "Maybe that's what a good Catholic education does for you," she chuckled. "But I agree, ghosts and spooky things like that never really crossed our minds."

"Until that night."

Their collective attitude has changed a bit since one fateful night on the dunes of Delaware Seashore State Park near Indian River Inlet.

"Now," said Jeff, with a cautious glance toward his wife, "we don't know what the heck to think of all of this."

"Don't ask me exactly where it happened," Jeff continued. "Gina and I always took long walks up and down the beach right around dark.

"As for me, it all started when I was about ten, and my parents bought this place over here. We lived in the city then, so I really cherished my time out here, and especially on the beach. I always felt some kinship with the ocean."

Jeff appears as a sensitive, articulate young man who would have no reason to concoct a tall tale for whatever purpose. In fact, he rejected any such notion.

"When Gina and I tell you our story," he said, "I frankly don't care if you believe me or not. You could drive away from here tonight laughing like hell at us two fools, but it will be you who will be the fools. Everything we will tell you happened just as we say, and I have to admit that if I was in your shoes, listening to us, I would probably drive away thinking it was all a bunch of hogwash. You just have to believe us that it is true, but don't ask how we could explain it rationally. Maybe that's your job."

Gina stared at her husband as he spoke, rolling her eyes occasionally as her memory connected with the words he spoke.

"Well, anyway, let's get into the events of that night," Jeff said.

"We had the place here for a week, and we did the usual. A little crabbing, some fishing and a whole lot of loafing and lounging in the sun. But our walks along the beach could not be denied. It didn't matter if it was pouring down rain or whatever, we felt that it was important to kind of keep up the tradition. Besides, it was a good walk, healthy, and a good way for a couple of city kids to commune with nature," Jeff smiled.

"I guess it was around ten o'clock that night, and the day was particularly clear and cool. Now, here's where it gets a little tricky. I almost hate to say this, but I really do believe it was a full moon that night, or at least very close to it," he said.

Gina interrupted: "Yeah," she said, "that makes the whole story suspect right from the start. You know, oooh-oooh, it was a dark and stormy night, etc., etc."

After Gina's whimsical interlude subsided, the strange story unfolded.

"OK, all I know that it was very clear and very bright that night," Jeff continued, "and there were only puffs of clouds over to the west, over land. Otherwise, it was a perfect, but a little chilly, night.

"On the horizon of the ocean, we saw some lights of ships or boats. Way, way up ahead, we saw some people walking north, the same direction Gina and I were walking. We remarked to each other how amazing it was that we seemed to have the beach all to ourselves.

"Along this one stretch were some pretty high dunes. Now, we had been looking up and down the beach and like I said, we were almost alone except for those other people way ahead of us. Well, all of a sudden, as if she just popped up out of nowhere, just a few yards ahead of us, was a young girl."

Jeff looked over at Gina, and from that point Gina took up the story.

"It was weird right from the start," she said. "Really, no sooner that we commented that we had the place to ourselves, we saw the woman, or girl. There seemed to be no way we could have missed seeing her as we looked up ahead. It was just in the couple of seconds that we looked at each other to say a few words that she appeared as if out of nowhere.

"Now, we didn't think anything was particularly ghostly about it," Gina continued, "but I think both of our hearts skipped a beat and I know for sure that I got a sudden rush of goosebumps.

"Well, we just walked along, ready to nod hello to the girl as we passed her. We had run out of things to say to each other, I guess, so we were both quiet."

"Maybe, Gina, we were both a little apprehensive," Jeff interjected.

"Yeah, I know I was a little confused," Gina replied.

"So there she was," Gina continued, "and it really was no big deal, I guess. But then, something even stranger happened.

"There was only a moderate surf that night, and, you know, it kept coming in but didn't make a whole lot of sound. No crashing waves, or anything like that.

"But all of a sudden, just off to our right, I heard a real, you know, violent sound coming from the water line. There was thumping, splashing, and even a whining and moaning sound. My very first reaction was that it was a big fish or a porpoise or something flapping around in the surf."

Jeff joined in, "Yeah, and I heard it, too. That's exactly what I thought. I know Gina and I looked at each other for a split second and I realized we both had heard the sounds, and then we looked over to where it was coming from.

"Sure enough, there was one small area of the beach and surf which was being churned up. Now remember that it was very clear that night, so we both saw it clear as a bell. There was splashing and thrashing and it looked as if there was nothing causing it," Jeff said.

"Again, nothing spooky registered with us until, sort of instinctively, we looked back to our left and to where the girl had been.

"She was still there," Jeff said, his voice becoming increasingly nervous, "but instead of sitting on the edge of a dune like she was when we first saw her, she was standing up."

Gina jumped into the conversation again: "I couldn't believe my eyes. I was scared too much to even move. It was like something out of a movie or something. Without a doubt, something was going on in the waves. In a flash, I imagined that it was someone struggling. A person, not a fish. Maybe someone was being pushed into the ocean, maybe someone was trying to save themself from drowning. Whatever the rational explanation, all that was missing was that someone or something. It was clear enough to see that there was apparently nothing causing the splashing and all the commotion.

"Within a second or so, I glanced back to the girl. I almost had to laugh, but I was too confused and, what's the word, enraptured, to do that. Like anything you would imagine in a scary story, this girl was standing very straight, with both arms extended toward us. For the first time, Jeff and I saw that she was wearing, now get this, one of those old-fashioned swimming suits. You know, like girls back in the early days of the century used to wear? That's exactly what she had on."

Fair enough. That's acceptable. But even the authors, fully seasoned after hundreds of interviews with people who say they have seen ghosts walking among us, were not quite prepared for what was to follow.

"She was standing there, just as Gina said," Jeff continued, "with her arms outstretched like in an old Dracula movie or something. I think, and neither Gina nor I can really recall exactly, but I think that the splashing sound ended. All I know is that our attention was riveted toward the girl.

"Well, as we watched this, Gina and I held hands very tightly and came very close together. I think I felt her hand shaking. Maybe it was mine.

"I guess I was first to notice it, so I whispered to Gina,

'doesn't it look as if she is, you know, transparent?' Gina didn't have to say anything. She just wrinkled her nose, sighed and shook her head up and down ever so slightly. "Then, we heard it. The girl started to talk. It was a low, very quiet 'help, help me . . . please help me.' "

Jeff asked for a break in the taping session so he could refill his soda glass and compose himself. Request granted.

Gina resumed the story. "Of course, I heard it too," she said. "It was very low and you could barely hear it above the natural sound of the ocean. But there was absolutely no doubt that here was a young girl, dressed in an old swimsuit, her arms pointing toward the sea, quietly asking 'he-e-lp . . . please help me.' You have to know that it was very frightening by that time."

Jeff was quick to point out that this entire episode took only a few minutes of real time. "Yeah," he responded, "but it seemed like Gina and I were frozen together out there for a lifetime."

Gina recounted the last seconds of the unearthly encounter. "There was no doubt that you could see right through her body," she affirmed. "As the time went on, and Jeff is right, it really didn't take long at all, but as the time went on she seemed to fade and fade a little more. I don't think she walked toward us, but I know it looked as if she was going to. But just about at the time she might have, she started to disappear. Now isn't that really hard to believe? She just faded into nothingness."

Heads of the interviewers and interviewees shook incredulously as silence followed Gina's concluding words.

Jeff added the final chapter to the story. "We have told this story to exactly three other people," he said. "Our closets friends, and my mother.

"My mother seemed to take it all in, and I think she believed us. She's that way. But our friends did exactly what we might have expected. They whoo'd and hooted and asked how much we had to drink that night. Believe me, we didn't have a drop that entire day. Lord knows, though, we had a stiff night cap when we finally got back to the house!"

Jeff and Gina cut their beach walk short that night. They went on beyond the dune into which the young girl seemed to fade, but their minds were no longer on a romantic, moon-drenched walk by the peaceful sea.

They lived with the memory of that night for three years, and it was only through a chance meeting with Jeff's mother that it was retold for this book.

They have not attempted to research any possible drowning of a young swimmer early in this century at that site. They are hard pressed to find the exact spot where the ghostly encounter took place.

They still spend many weeks of the year at their family's Indian River Bay retreat, and still take long, leisurely strolls on the beach.

But now, they keep wary ears trained on the surf and on each dune they pass.

"Now that we have had the initial experience," Jeff said, "I guess we have had our baptism.

"This may sound strange," he continued as he reached for Gina's hand, "but now that we went through that — and I have to admit that despite all I was taught and all I ever believe it was a ghost we saw that night — after what we saw and heard, I sort of wish that lonely, tragic young woman would show up again. This sounds strange, I know, but in those few minutes, I felt that I got to know that girl. Who knows, maybe if it was only to put her soul to rest, we could help her the next time."

PHANTOMS OF THE FORTS

Throughout the history of the Delaware Bay, military minds have seen fit to fortify the shores of the capes and the bay against whomever the enemy may have been at the time.

One of the most incredible "finds" the authors came across in the course of their research for this book was the ominous, awesome presence of Fort Saulsbury, a relic of World War I which remains essentially intact deep within a very private farm near Slaughter Beach.

The good folks at the historic Mispillion Lighthouse directed the researchers to the old fort. Try as Suzanne Racz of Mispillion could, she could not ferret any ghostly tales out of the long life of what is the only surviving wood frame lighthouse in Delaware.

She ventured, however, that if any place nearby would have a ghost story attached to it, it was likely to be the big bunker of Fort Saulsbury.

Fort Saulsbury. Many, if not most people in the area may never have heard of the place, and couldn't place it if they had.

And yet, it is a site which is well worth preserving as a state, and perhaps national historic landmark.

Inching beyond the "No Trespassing" signs that frame the dirt road which leads to the farm and fort, the flat fields and clumps of woods which surround the property belie the magnitude that is within.

At once, as the road makes a turn toward a cluster of low, frame buildings, a giant hulk of concrete emerges and towers over the landscape. Several hundred yards beyond this first behemoth looms yet another.

The fort, which was named for Willard Saulsbury, a Delaware senator, was erected in 1917 as part of the government's hasty and, as it became obvious in this case, hapless home defenses against the German threat during the first world war.

Fort Saulsbury was placed so far up the bay and inland because the army felt it would be more secure and out of range of shipboard enemy guns.

Fortunately for the world but unfortunately for Fort Saulsbury, World War I ended before construction of the installation was completed. Forty-feet long, twelve-inch calibre guns placed on carriages were in place, and both could fire four-feet long, one-ton shells at a range of more than twenty miles.

Their services were never needed.

The guns were fired first in a 1921 test. It was nine years later that they were again fired, and at that time the government learned a lesson from the first firing.

Perhaps the authorities never counted on it, or factored it in their calculations, but when the powerful guns were shot, the repercussions rattled homes, shattered windows and sent nearby poultry flocks into a tizzy.

For the 1930 test, the army gave fair warning, said it would pay for any broken eggs as the result of the test.

In the wake of more than a dozen blasts of the big twelve-inchers, it is said that most windows in most homes in a wide area were broken.

Through the 1930s, the fort was virtually dormant. Just before the outbreak of the second world war, the guns of Fort Saulsbury were relocated to Fort Miles, on Cape Henlopen. Four two-story barracks buildings, an infirmary, recreation hall, storehouse and administration building were built near the bunkers of Fort Saulsbury in 1940, and the facility was garrisoned by the 261st Coast Artillery Battery B.

Still, Fort Miles took the forefront as the primary

defensive fortification of Cape Henlopen. Fort Saulsbury was to find a more useful purpose.

Up and down the Delaware coast, from New Castle to Bethany Beach, Italian and German prisoners-of-war were interned at small POW camps. Fort Saulsbury, with its substantial walls and remote location, was a natural setting for such a camp.

After this service was carried out, the fort was once again idled and virtually abandoned, and by 1946 was officially designated as inactive and surplus.

Experts on American fortifications consider the fort to be the only surviving World War I-era fort which is virtually un-altered and in its primitive state.

The bunkers and their magazines have been converted into refrigeration units and pickle storage vaults over the years, and more recently, the owners of the land have stored boats and other equipment inside one of them, but they do remain almost intact. While the present tenants of the land have found good use for the massive bunkers, they have been careful not to destroy the integrity of the structures.

In fact, cells from the POW days still line the front bunker, and what was the prisoners' bathrooms is still remarkably well preserved.

There is some graffiti on the walls, but it is the work of the prisoners who passed through the fort. The dim vestiges of paint and sketchings are reminders of the time when thousands of enemy soldiers inhabited the big bunker.

According to some people, there may be less obvious and much more elusive evidence that some past residents of Fort Saulsbury may never have left.

One of the tenants present at the time of this writing did not deny that the dark, dank corridors, the cramped cells and musty washrooms in what was the POW section of the fort may be haunted.

"A girl who used to come around here used to say strange things would happen here," that tenant said.

She continued: "We used to walk through here at night, scare each other and that. But one night, she had a premonition about this one particular slate back in one of the back bunkers. The bathroom stalls are all separated by these big, incredibly heavy slate panels.

"One of the slates fell on that girl, but she was able to actually lift it off herself. She said she felt a superhuman force helping her. I don't know if that's anything ghostly, but it sure was strange."

Unbeknownst to that tenant, one of the "researchers" who visited her and her husband that day was also a medium. He would be able to "read" any kind of psychic messages that may be emitted from whatever spirit would dwell in the bunker.

And read, he did!

"There is nothing malevolent here," the medium assured the writer. "But there is a fairly strong presence. It seems to be centered in the area of the cells. Yes, this is a sort of spiral of energy that indicates what one would call a 'ghost.'"

In a series of flash messages, the medium detected numbers, letters, colors and emotions: "I sense the numerals six and nine . . . red and green . . . the letters M and K . . . I feel not sadness, but dejection . . . strange as it seems, and I know the story of this place, but I feel homesickness, and I feel that language is a problem, or at least different."

Such is the typical "reading" of an alleged haunted building. It is felt by many who study the paranormal that, as outlined elsewhere in this volume, that certain bits of information passed on by the energy of a departed intelligent life do indeed become etched into a building or environmental feature in some as yet unexplained and unconfirmed way.

Fort Saulsbury may or may not be haunted, in the classical sense of the word. It is, though, by all indications, awash in some level of psychic activity detectable by some minds which are either blessed or cursed with the ability to communicate with the "other side."

40

The old bunkers are certainly haunted by those who are still alive and have passed through its concrete portals. Memories of jaunty "bombing runs" by prankster pilots out of Dover Air Force Base who once strafed German prisoners with soda pop bottles dropped from low-flying planes onto the prison grounds; memories of training sessions, droll duty and yes, even memories of working in the pickle plant. It is an historic, vital part of Sussex County (and in some way, American) history.

Another Delaware Bay fort has been preserved and is a popular spot for summer visitors who enjoy picnicking in and around it and enjoying the bounty of nature which surrounds it.

The 178-acre Pea Patch Island is straddled by the coasts of Delaware and New Jersey, some fifteen miles south of Wilmington. It is at Pea Patch where the river becomes a bay.

The island is so named because of a shipwreck legend. An 18th century barkentine, it is said, went aground on a tiny sandbar and spilled its cargo of peas on the little patch of land. The pea vines took root and an island was born.

This improbably tale sets the stage for the long and storied history of the island and its sole occupant, the imposing Fort Delaware.

The fort consumes only about six acres of the island, but when it was completed just prior to the Civil War, it was the largest fort in the nation — larger even than Fort Sumter.

Actually, an idea for a bastian of defense on the island came along as early as 1794, when noted District of Columbia planner Pierre L'Enfant recommended fortifications on what he curiously called Pip Ash Island. His suggestion fell on deaf ears.

The federal government managed to make it through the War of 1812 with no major Delaware Bay installations, but by 1823 the military decided to heed L'Enfant's earlier call.

This first earthen recoubt was destroyed, rebuilt, destroyed again and rebuilt again. In the meantime, the nation made it through another was, with Mexico, without substantial protection on the bay.

Ironically, the current structure was ordered built by U.S. Secretary of War Jefferson Davis, who later became commander-in-chief of the Confederate army and navy.

That is ironic because the fort's chief claim to fame was its tenure as a prisoner-of-war camp. Built by paid and slave labor (at between 40 cents to $1.25 a day wages), the heavily armed fort's garrisons never fired a shot in hostility, and instead housed thousands of Confederate prisoners during the war between the states.

At one time, crude barracks and related structures spread out over the length and breadth of the island. At the peak of activity, more than 12,500 prisoners were confined there.

At first, "rebel" prisoners escaped the island as if wriggling through a sieve. Dozens, and then hundreds of inmates found their way out, until more guards and patrol boats wee deployed to control the situation.

Some have called Fort Delaware the "Andersonville of the North." Most records show, however, that conditions on the island were far better than its Confederate counterpart.

Prisoners participated in debates, concerts, lecture series and even published their own hand-written newsletter. Still, there were complaints. "The granite walls are wet with moisture, the stone floors damp and cold, and the air is impure," wrote one prisoner. If he would visit the site today, he would find that not much has changed.

The prisoners were released in 1866, and by 1870 the fort was all but abandoned. In 1897, major renovations were made, and with a main battery of 12 and 16-inch guns, the fort became a kind of stationary battleship anchored in the bay.

The fort was later manned, "just in case," during World War I and was part of the coastal defense system which included Fort Saulsbury.

By the second world war, it was determined that Fort Delaware had outlived its military usefulness and was relegated to being a base for mining operations in the bay. The fort was abandoned after World War II and fell prey to scavengers and vandals. In 1951, it was cleaned up and public tours opened three years later.

The building has really changed little since its Civil War days. Surrounded by a 30-foot moat, the massive walls of the pentagonal structure are broken by long, narrow, vertical windows and gun ports.

Inside is what some consider the finest example of brick arch masonry in the country. An estimated 25 million bricks wrap around in graceful curved ceilings and portals.

Throughout the dark, dismal chambers of the fort are reminders of its past. Prisoners' names are scrawled into the plaster. Cannons and remains of the gun mountings are still in place. Timbers, weakened by time and the ravages of bay weather, barely cling to architectural soundness.

The administration building is crude and somewhat foreboding. The old cells and bunkrooms are stark examples of what was the best of life at the prison. These remaining areas in the fort itself were where the top brass of the prisoner ranks were held captive. Enlisted men were housed in wooden barracks built on flimsy wetland where vermin and poison contributed to the deaths of more than 2,700 of the prisoners. Today, it is said that the sounds of chains dragging through the dungeons and ramparts, oars sloshing in the waters around the fort and the moans of dying men can be heard.

Park Ranger Ramon Armstrong confirmed that he has seen what he believes to be incontrovertible evidence that at least one of the alleged spirits has been captured on film.

One visitor, Armstrong said, took a Polaroid picture of a companion positioned in a darkened archway. The photograph clearly depicted the photographer's friend, but quite visible just over the friend's shoulder in the picture was the wispy silhouette of a Confederate soldier.

Ranger Armstrong, who told his story in a 1986 interview, tends to buck the official line, which essentially debunks any notion that ghosts infest the fort. Still, he is not alone in his assertion.

Another man, a volunteer at Fort Delaware, said he would tell his tale if his name was not mentioned in the book.

"No doubt about it," he started, "there's ghosts in here. I've seen them, and I know two others who have reported seeing or hearing unearthly things in this fort. No doubt about it.

"One time, three of us were wandering around on our own, over in the passageway that leads to what they call the dungeons. As far as I knew, we were almost alone on the island at the time. There were some others traipsing around, but they were over by the sally port, across the parade ground. Anyway, we were just lollygagging around when we heard some chatter and clatter coming from inside the old ammunition rooms they used for solitary confinement for the prisoners. I mean, it sounded like a couple of guys, or maybe even more than a couple, were laughing and whooping and hollering back in there. No doubt about it.

"That was crazy, because we knew there was nobody in there. Still, we braced ourselves and decided to go check up. You know, we had heard rumors of ghosts before, and each of us had gotten strange feelings at some time or another in there, but this was really scary because it was so obvious."

The man from New Castle continued his story, and pointed out that he had always been interested in the supernatural, and that fact may have tainted his attitude.

"This ghost stuff has always interested me," he continued, "ever since I was a kid in Wilmington. They used to say the old church down by the Christiana where I grew up had ghosts all over it. Indians, old soldiers and others. Of course, I would always go down to the old graveyard and see what I could see. Never really saw anything, but sure as hell got scared a lot just thinking about what I might see!

"I know exactly what I saw that time in the fort, though, and those other two guys would back me up. We all saw it, and heard it. First it was the ruckus in the dungeon and then, within a blink, we saw shadowy figures darting about down the corridor toward the cell. No doubt about it. They were all wearing those Johnny Reb hats on their heads, and we knew that what we were watching were the ghosts of Confederate soldiers back in those cells. No doubt about it."

The man, whose distinctive "Dulwor" accent and choice of expletives have been cleaned up, said he and his companions heard the "ruckus" for about two minutes. The shadowy figures with the "Johnny Reb" hats appeared only momentarily, but each of the men would, in the words of their spokesman, "swear on a stack of five Bibles" that every word he spoke was the "galldarn truth."

No doubt about it.

TALES OF TREASURE
AND TREACHERY

What would any book about ghosts and legends of any shore be without a smattering of stories of pirates, buried treasure and dastardly deeds on the sea and on land?

Cape Henlopen, the Delaware Bay and the Coast of Delaware are rife with such sagas, and some of the best-known names in piracy are mentioned among those who have contributed to the intrigue.

Such tales date to 1630, when Capt. David Pietersen DeVries came in search of great whales which were said to inhabit the waters off the cape. The first band of settlers numbered 28, and their compound, at what they called Bloemert's Kil, was almost immediately destroyed by Indians. A monument on Pilottown Road in Lewes marks the spot of the massacre.

This tragic episode not only set the stage for the eventual permanent settlement on Cape Henlopen, but also was a precursor of many bloody events which would befall the people of the Delaware shores.

Noted Sussex County historian Hazel Brittingham, whose exhaustive research and perseverance has led to many published articles about the county's development, counts among her most cherished folk tales of the area one that many not have ghostly overtones, but certainly has a supernatural aura about it.

The story is set on Christmas Eve, 1673, when the British forces led by Captain Thomas Howell (acting on behalf of Lord Baltimore) swept into the Dutch settlement of Whore Kill Towne.

Capt. Howell was ordered to attack the village which is now known as Lewes and surprise the residents. He and his men were to totally destroy every building, capture all boats and round up every gun and all ammunition. The move was the continuation of a bitter struggle between British and Dutch interests for control of the Cape Henlopen region.

The British troops had no problem routing the villagers. While no human casualties were reported in the siege, every building was systematically put to the torch.

Every building but one.

Facing the total destruction of his settlement, one man reportedly pleaded with Captain Howell to allow one building to remain as a shelter for refugees, and especially a handful of pregnant women who would be turned out into the bitter December cold after the ruthless action of the soldiers.

The snide captain challenged not the mortal, but God himself to provide such salvation. If God could prevent that one building from being burned to the ground, he said, then the settlers would find their shelter.

That one building chosen by the cunning captain was a thatch-roof barn. While all around it buildings flared up and disintegrated in burning embers, that one barn seemed to refuse to ignite.

In amazement, Captain Howell, his British troops and the Dutch settlers watched as time after time, torch after torch, the seemingly fragile and flammable barn remained undamaged.

Divine intervention prevailed. A dazzled and humbled Howell bowed to the desires of the diety and backed away from the unscathed barn.

As the British troops returned to tell of their triumph, the folks of Whore Kill walked solemnly into the barn to spend what could be considered a night of a miracle on Cape Henlopen.

Other stories from the earliest days of life on Cape Henlopen and in Sussex County are not nearly as fortuitous in nature.

From the time pirates were first noticed off the capes of Delaware and New Jersey sometime around 1685, it was literally war against the marauders.

Settlers were urged and later ordered to strengthen their individual and collective guards against the plunderers who arrived in sloops and schooners.

Raids throughout the 1690s threatened the citizens of Lewistown, or Lewes, and toward the end of that decade a system of drum signals alerted people that buccaneers were on their way.

In 1698, more than four dozen daring men rowed to shore and proceeded to terrorized the village. This raid was attributed to a ne'er-do-well named Canoot, but a more recognizable name was mentioned within a short time following that incident.

Captain Kidd, alternately called a pirate and a patriot, called on Lewes in the spring of 1700. It is generally accepted that at that time of William Kidd's sailing career, he was a legitimate businessman. It is widely rumored, though, that while Kidd displayed this facade, he was indeed involved in some untoward activity on the high seas and in remote ports, and he used his courtesy as a cover for more secretive dealings.

There are rumors, too, that Captain Kidd may have buried some of his vast treasures in the dunes of Cape Henlopen. Then again, such rumors of Captain Kidd treasure surface about every five miles up and down the east coast.

Another notorious name associated with the "golden age" of piracy, Blackbeard, is also associated with the Delaware shores.

Born William Teach, the corsair known for his ribbon-bedecked beard (14 knots for 14 wives, it was said), reportedly sailed off Cape Henlopen in about 1717. There are flimsy rumors that even he buried treasure somewhere along the Delaware Bay coastline.

To that effect, legends persist that the treasure lies somewhere deep in the soil along Black Bird Creek, Delaware. Some even put forth the notion that Black Bird is really "Black Beard," and the stream was named for the pirate.

Folklorist Kim Burdick, who has collected hundreds of stories from Delawareans, wrote of a former Milford mayor who recalled a story told by his grandfather.

Ham McNatt's grandfather claimed that the ghost of a headless pirate directed him to some of Blackbeard's buried booty. Once he determined that the spook had led him to the treasure site, he marked it and aimed to return under a full moon to dig up the fortune.

Return he did, dig he did, and all was going well until he looked up to see the ghostly pirate. Struck by unimaginable fear, and being attacked by the sword-wielding, decapitated wraith, he ran to save himself.

After he had gained enough courage to return the following day, he found that the treasure chest he had actually reached the night before was gone, as was the ghost.

In the archives of the Delaware Folklore Society is the testimony of one H. Lloyd Jones, Jr., who wrote of his grandmother's recollection of the rotting timbers of a schooner which was half-buried in the muddy bottom of shallow Black Bird Creek during the 1860s. Her father told her it was the scuttled ship of Blackbeard.

Throughout the early years of the eighteenth century, pirates dominated the tavern talk and teased the consciousness of citizens along the Delaware coast.

More than one thousand raiders were reported off the eastern seaboard, and the government finally realized that the problem was widespread enough and serious enough to take stronger measures of protection.

Taxes were levied and defenses were strengthened to deal with the pirate threat, and by the mid-1700s serious piracy off the Delaware coast had all but disappeared.

During those adventurous years, it is generally accepted that at least one Delawarean, Levi West, was able to capitalize on the laxity of the authorities' ability to control piracy.

West, who supposedly marred his cheeks with the backfiring of muskets, went by the pseudonym of Blueskin, and operated his vessel out of Rehoboth Bay.

Did any of these pirates actually leave hordes of jewels, gold and silver behind — perhaps buried deep in the sand or soil?

No one has ever proven there is buried treasure along the Delaware shore. Oddly enough, however, a personage none other than William Penn himself once reported to local authorities in Lewes that a handful of men from that town had boarded the vessel of Captain Kidd and had taken from it certain valuables which they spirited onto shore without paying the proper taxes. Penn indicated his informer felt the perpertrators, who had removed the money and goods with the consent of the pirate, may have stashed the loot somewhere.

A token investigation by the chief law enforcement officer and tax collector in Lewes was fruitless.

There are other speculative tales that other sailors slipped off Kidd's ship with treasure chests and strong boxes, buried them in the dunes of Cape Henlopen, and died before they could retrieve them.

In random conversations in the watering holes of Lewes and Milford, there is still talk of those who have had encounters with ghostly visions of pirates on the beaches of the ocean and bay, but none of these idle stories has much substance.

There is, of course, the recurring story of the ghost schooner of Lewes Creek. And, should you be brave enough to wander along a certain stretch of beach near Roosevelt Inlet, and should all conditions be right, you may catch a chilling glimpse of the most famous of the phantom vessels said to rise from the waves offshore.

They say it is the very ship of Captain Kidd which can be seen under full four-masted canvas, returning in an eternal quest for an elusive fortune hidden somewhere in the soil of Sussex.

Secret stashes are a vital part of Sussex County folklore. Author Dorothy Pepper wrote of the widow Zippy Lewis who, rumor had it, buried a good amount of gold in the dunes near Fenwick Island. And, according to historian Virginia Cullen, homes on Second Street and Market Street in Lewes are, or have been, gorged with fortunes ferreted into walls and floorboards by eccentric former owners.

As "phantom ships" go, however, none is as noteworthy as that of the legendary British sloop deBraak, which went down in a Cape Henlopen gale on May 25, 1798.

Historians concede that the rigging of the top-heavy Dutch-built, British-rigged ship was the reason the 125-foot vessel capsized that day.

Those more inclined toward the supernatural would like to accept the time-honored story that it was not faulty seamanship or design that sank the deBraak, but the irresistible lure of the Bad Weather Witch.

All conditions must be right for the ghostly re-enactment of the sinking of the deBraak. It will sail on smooth water under a full moon overhead. It will be silent, positioned just off the point of Cape Henlopen, and will appear very, very real.

Perhaps the mournful sound of gagging, screaming sailors will waft through the sudden breeze which will cast an icy chill. Perhaps you will hear the creaking of the deBraak's timbers as they twist and contort in the dying throes of those final minutes.

Within a scant moment, which will seem timeless to you, it will be over. The wind will cease, the moon will be shrouded by a cloud, and the unearthly sounds which echoed over the sea will be silenced. You will have experienced the sinking of the HMS deBraak.

Legends beget legends, and the tale of the ghostly deBraak, the sinister Bad Weather Witch and the treasure it may guard have spurned new and intriguing versions of time-honored tales.

Kim Burdick, the premier folklorist of Wilmington, touched on a fantastic story which has Captain James

Drew, of the ill-fated deBraak, rising from his grave in St. Peter's church in Lewes and wandering the beach looking for his ship and dead sailors.

It is also Burdick who, in her 1984 play, "Delaware Ghosts," penned a warning to those who might seek to disturb the Bad Weather Witch in its lair:

Don't touch the deBraak,
ye vermin and swine —
Her bow is my cradle,
her treasures are mine!

But just what treasures were being guarded by the old witch beneath the waves?

After nearly two centuries of searching, the deBraak, she of untold fortunes and precious cargo, was hastily and foolishly raised by salvagers who plucked the delicate remains from the sandy bottom as a child would pluck a clam shell from the wet sand.

Alas, the only fortune to be found on the deBraak was in historical terms. Important artifacts, preserved fairly well by the cold, deep water, emerged to tell new stories of life aboard an 18th century British warship. But fortunes in gold and silver, there were none.

Blame the Bad Weather Witch, they say.

The sorceress of the sea has been blamed for the inability of mere mortals to retrieve the wealth from the deBraak since the first mortal dragged the bottom in search of that wealth.

In 1935, an expedition led by Charles Colstad and Richard Wilson was one of the best-financed failures in the search for the deBraak treasure. So frustrated by the failure were some of the salvagers that they actually fabricated an effigy of the Bad Weather Witch, blasted it with rounds of gunfire, burned it and tossed it overboard.

Nice try.

For the book, "Shipwrecks, Sea Stories and Legends of the Delaware Coast," the authors of this volume caught up with a kind of renegade diver who once — only once — made a dive near the soggy, sagging timbers of the deBraak several years ago.

His name was Jack, and he confirmed for us in sober, somber detail, "there really is something weird going on down there, and it's because of that damned witch!"

He continued, "I don't even believe in witches and goblins and stuff like that, but when it comes to the deBraak, I'd bet my last dollar that there's some kind of curse attached to the wreck. I don't know who did it, or why, but somebody put a curse on that boat.

"I know that when I dove down near her one time, legally and all, I saw something that scared the hell out of me. It wasn't a witch or a monster or anything I could describe, but there was a really strange kind of glow and a big air bubble as I remember. I got the hell out of there right quick. I never went back. In fact, I pity anybody who does. I swear, that ship is cursed.

"Now, I'm not a crazy man. But maybe it's just me who's cursed. This'll sound strange to you, but you know what? It's so bad that one time I went to the (Zwaanendael) museum, and I saw the captain's trunk and hull model of the deBraak and all the other things that they had there. Well, I got a tingling feeling inside. Heh, heh, when I left the museum, just outside the door of the place, I tripped and fell flat on my face. Now I'm not saying the Water Witch did that, but it was really crazy."

Crazy it was, Jack. But just as unfathomable is yet another story which attributes a phantom ship just off the shore of Port Mahon, on the bay.

It surfaces, they say, just off Port Mahon, near Little Creek. And again, it's best you stand on the beach under a full moon for the full effect of this horrid vision.

Horrid it is because the corpse of the ship owner, Joshua McCowan, dangles from a rope on the bowsprit.

McCowan (or, in some accounts, McGowan) was slain by a member of his crew who was jealous of his romance with Sally Stout, a comely lass whose father was a governor of Delaware in the early 19th century.

The body of the captain can be seen silhouetted in the moon-illuminated sky, according to old-timers — some who will swear they have seen it themselves!

Ted Abrams, a Baltimore man who has spent many summers on the Delaware shore, tells yet another story of a ghostly image he claims to have witnessed on two occasions just off Broadkill Beach.

"It all started out innocently enough," Abrams said. "I was about fourteen years old, and my grandfather and I were sitting on a dune shooting the breeze. I happened to look out into the bay and saw the lights of a ship heading up toward Philly.

"Now, that was nothing unusual, of course. But between the beach and that ship were other lights. They weren't quite as distinct, and although there was some sort of a central light or whatever, they seemed to be fuzzy and seemed to be glowing, maybe you'd call them phosphorescent."

Ted continued, saying he stared at the lights for several seconds, trying to figure out what they might have been before alerting his grandfather to their presence.

"It really was a little out of the ordinary," he said. "I had seen all kinds of lights out there, but nothing quite like these. They bobbed on the water, and there was nothing distinguishable about them at all.

"So, my grandfather was just sitting there, there was a lull in whatever we were talking about. I quietly pointed the lights out to him. I didn't want him to think I was off my rocker. Sure enough, he saw them, too. At least that let me know I wasn't going nuts.

"He straightened up, squinted, and slumped back. He whispered to me, 'Tedd-o, them's what you call corpse lights!' "

Tedd-o, as his father and grandfather called him, arched his eyebrows. "Corpse lights? I wondered if he was joking, or just trying to scare me. Whatever, when he said it, I got a chill.

"Then, he really got me. He told me that when he was sailing on an old skipjack years before, they'd see those kind of lights from time to time. He said they were the lights of the ghost of a seaman who had drowned at that precise location. It was the spirit of the dead man shining through the water, he said. Only when conditions were just right would it happen."

Ted still shudders as he talks about the experience. He said the second time he saw similar lights was in the Mediterranean Sea off Sicily. Standing watch on the deck of a Navy destroyer with two other sailors, he pointed out the lights and explained to them what his grandfather had told him. "After their laughter died down," Ted recalled, "I realized that they thought I had lost it."

Not to be the one who turns the cold water on Ted's hot shower, but his grandfather's "corpse lights" just may have a scientific explanation.

Throughout the history of man's sailing on the seas, similar sights have been reported. They have emerged in seafaring jargon as dozens of entities, from St. Elmo's Fire to La Feu des Gabiers to the strikingly similar Cuerpo Santo or Corposant.

Some say the lights portent danger or evil. The flickering glow has been attributed to insects, oil, the natural chemical reaction of certain gases and substances in or on the sea, and Satan.

The connection with the Devil has been traced to French legend that tells of Satan's ship of the dead. Doomed and damned souls collected as the Devil's crew cried and groaned in eternal agony, and the sound amused Lucifer. Hearing the mournful sound would occasionally cause the evil one to break into a sinister cackling.

The Devil's laughter enraged St. Elmo, who in a fit of anger attempted to sink the ship. The Devil lashed back and sparked a raging fire which stopped St. Elmo in his tracks. This fire, according to this legend, still blazes on the surface of the sea from time to time, place to place.

The sea, and in this case, the bay, has always guarded its secrets with a vengeance. With all the pirate activity, the numerous shipwrecks and the untold tales of treasure which swirl around the Delaware coast, no one can be sure exactly what fortunes rest on the bottom of the Delaware Bay.

Nelson Vanaman, who was 93 years old at the time of this writing, is a Wilmington native who started his working life as a freight conductor on the Reading Railroad and wound up running fishing party boats along the shore of the bay.

In his mobile home in Bowers Beach, Nelson recalled with fondness the clam and crab dredging his boats, "Bob White" and "Morning Star" would undertake, and remembered one incident which still baffles him.

"We were down below Big Stone Beach," he said, "in that deep water. Every once in a while, we'd dredge up a rock that would have streaks of yellow. There used to be a mechanic down here who once said, 'I believe that's gold.'

"Well, a captain on a boat didn't want to haul that stuff. He had a big pile of it and he'd throw it overboard. One time, though, Frankie Gennero picked up a big rock with the yellow streak and said that he was going to keep it.

"He took it to his shop, ground it up and sent a sample to the assay office in Washington. It came back that it was solid gold.

"They wanted to know where he got it and how much there was of it. But, these old oystermen, they thought it was all baloney.

"Well, old Frankie found out there was gold down there. The one chunk he saved didn't have nearly as many streaks as many others that were tossed overboard.

"I often wondered if some years ago a boat that sank off there might have gone down with gold. Every once in a while, you'd pick up a rock and you'd see these yellow streaks of ore."

Nelson sat back and pondered those days and that gold. "It's down there in about 75 feet of water, down there where those big tankers lay in," he continued. "I don't know how it got there, or how much there is, but's there. I'd like to have just what I've seen tossed overboard. I'd be a rich man today, I'll tell you that!"

THE HENLOPEN DEVIL

This story, we hope, will be fun to read. That's all.

In the quest for ghost stories and such along the Delaware Coast, one is prone to meet those who dabble in tall tales and stretches of the imagination. It remains for the reader to sort out the wheat of truth from the chaff of fable.

Some folks take great pleasure, and are quite crafty at building a boulder out of a grain of fact.

There are some who would include Cape Henlopen, and indeed the entire Delaware seacoast, within the Bermuda Triangle of lost ships and planes fame.

Granted, the Coast Guard was baffled by the total disappearance of a giant C-133 cargo plane which was last seen 60 miles off the Delaware coast in 1963, and several pleasure boats, fishing vessels and freighters have slipped under the waves without a trace over the years. But to call the Delaware shore a stretch of the mysterious zone of death and disappearance is a bit daring.

One man who makes no bones whatsoever about piling legend upon legend is Mike Kennedy, the naturalist at Cape Henlopen State Park.

While it may be difficult to link any "Devil's Triangle" calamaties with the Delaware coast, it is conceivable — just conceivable — that the frightening Jersey Devil could have made its way to the shores of Delaware.

Fact of fiction, the bizarre creature has made an impact in Delaware and even Cape Henlopen. In the Bowers Maritime Museum, there are several sketches of impressions of the creature.

One is by Millard Thompson, who went on to the House of Representatives in the 1940s.

When he was a student at the Saxon School, a Methodist church school near Bowers, Thompson recorded his concept of the Jersey Devil.

"It was cloven-hoofed," he noted, "a long-tailed thing with the head of a collie dog, the face of a horse, wings of a bat, body of a kangaroo — half human, half animal."

Mike Kennedy is one of those responsible for keeping the lore and legend of Cape Henlopen alive through imaginative programs at the state park. Nature may be his profession, but the supernatural is among his passions.

Adept at explaining the habits and habitats of the flora, fauna, fish and fowl of the cape to both children and adults alike, Kennedy takes particular pleasure in, at least during the Halloween season, telling the tale of the Henlopen Devil. He has had some accomplices, too.

As Kennedy tells it, the cackling, howling, foul monster which tormented the folks and flocks of the Jersey Shore, Pine Barrens and beyond, made its way to Cape Henlopen on the ice floes of a nearly-frozen Delaware Bay a long time ago.

It is believed that the monster found a mate, and the resulting offspring was born somewhere near Gordon Pond. It was every bit as ugly and sinister as its parent, and came to be known by whoever caught a glimpse of it as the Cape Henlopen Devil.

Imagine, if you will, the wide eyes and ashen faces of young people gathered around a sand dune on a cool summer evening. Kennedy speaks in hushed tones. He speaks of the beast that may be lurking just beyond the dunes, or just around the bend. It is, he confides to the children, a beast that groans and then howls and then shrieks and squeals in pitches high enough to shake the dead from their graves.

The children are told of how the Devil's eyes glow at night. They glow red, yellow, orange — fiery and piercing are this monster's eyes. And, they are assured, it could be watching them at that very moment!

No sooner does Kennedy set a mood charged with anticipation and fear does he announce to the young folks that this macabre Devil has indeed crossed their path that very night. And sure enough, it has been snared and held in captivity by Kennedy's worthy assistant.

The mood changes. Will the children actually see this monster? Will they have the bejeebers scared out of them when its hideous presence is revealed?

After several more moments of stage-setting, along comes the star of this scary show. Paws crush the sand. A wheezing, throaty groan can be heard. There are horns on its head. Its face is twisted and contorted. It is, Kennedy assures them, the dread Henlopen Devil!!

As the children shift uneasily in their positions, out trots Eric Pearson, a volunteer at the state park. With him is the "Devil." The Devil's name is Sam. Sam is a plump, squat, nine year-old pet pug of Eric Pearson's, and certainly not monstrous in any way.

But with a couple of crude, hand-made horns on its head, and with its asthmatic breathing difficulties, little Sam certainly provides some moments of surprise for the youngsters.

Actually, a dog plays a key role in a famous, ferocious ghost that haunts a stretch of Route 12 between Frederica and Felton.

The best time to witness the raucous romping of what is known as the Fence Rail Dog is during a thunderstorm. But according to time-honored testimonies, you would probably not want to meet up with this ghastly ghost.

Dog-like and "as long as a fence rail," according to a story repeated in a Federal Writers Project book of the 1930s, the creature has eyes that glow a flaming red and a "great bushy tail up over its back."

Some contend that the black mongrel is actually the ghost of a murderer who disposed of the body of his servant victim by mashing it with the corn. It is the killer's spirit, legend has it, that somehow turned into the flaming-eyed, giant dog.

Its name is not Sam.

That dog, incidentally, that "Fence Rail Dog," occupies a region populated with several other spirits. The 1777 home known as Mordington, along McColley Pond, is haunted.

It is haunted, the story goes, by the spirit of a beautiful young woman known as "Tom's daughter."

Nobody is certain who "Tom" was, but the story handed down the decades is that the girl was a light-skinned slave who was confined to an upstairs room of the mansion after she resisted the amorous advances of her master.

Facing a lonely life and the threat of the overseer, the girl opted to open a window in the room and leap to her death on the lawn far below.

This spirit, it is said, still walks the grounds of old Mordington, and the sound of her agonized moans, screams and her death-dealing fall can be heard from time to time.

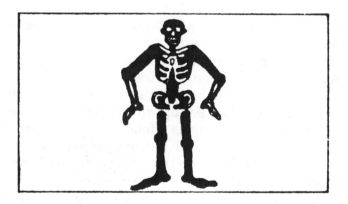

THE FACE IN THE MIRROR

Legends are one thing. "They say" that "under a full moon" the "phantom" "stalks the woods" on the "anniversary of the murder."

All elements fall neatly into place for a chilling, perhaps thrilling account of a brush with the unexplained. It makes for good reading and in a very true sense contributes to the heritage and texture of a people and a region. A land without a legend is somehow empty and unfulfilled.

It is something altogether different, however, when a ghost story hits home. When one encounters a very real, face to face (so to speak) meeting with a member of the other side, the "they say" stories become somehow irrelevant.

Face it. Who would you tell if you actually "saw a ghost?" Who would you trust so explicitly to not break into laughter or question your sanity after they were told by you that you had seen, heard, felt or even sensed a spirit.

We enclose "saw a ghost" in quotation marks not in mockery or doubt but because the mere thought of doing so is out of the realm of possibility and probability for most people.

But it happens, and it happens more frequently than most folks might imagine. And it happens to everyday people up and down the Delaware coast.

As a young girl in her King's Highway home, Holly Downs never thought she would one day explain to people a peculiar episode that has her baffled to this day.

Holly's mother, Arden Nagy, said she also felt a presence in the lovely home to the rear of the fire hall in Lewes.

She never saw anything in the seventeen years she lived in the place, but she believed that there was something not "haunting" the house but certainly cohabitating with them.

Haunting is such a harsh word anyway. It conjures up eerie spectres, rattling chains and things that go bump in the night.

Things went bump in the night in the Nagy home a few years ago, and there are indications that some of those bumps continue to this day. But anyone who has listened to the rattling of pots and pans or watched as a box slowly creeps across the attic floor has agreed that the spirit in the King's Highway house is benevolent.

Holly remembered the times odd things would happen to her as a young child in the house. She and her mother would dismiss them as happenstance, the creaking and rattling of the house, or whatever other rational explanation they could come up with at the time.

But some things could not be written off as quickly.

One night in her upstairs bedroom, Holly was going about her business alone when she felt the gentle pressure of a hand moving her to the side. "It was as if a hand was on my shoulder, like when somebody brushes past you. I definitely felt something I couldn't explain," said Holly.

Out of reflex, she looked for her mother. Her mother was nowhere near.

On another occasion, young Holly was biding her time in her parents' room when her eyes were distracted toward the dresser mirror. "I looked up," she said, "and in an instant there was a face in the mirror. It was turned to the side, and it just went by and moved across the mirror."

She nervously glanced around the room after the phantom silhouette flashed through the mirror. She was, as she had known, alone.

There were other unexplained occurrences, Holly said. She and others would hear footsteps slowly tracking across upstairs rooms and corridors where nobody was, and from time to time objects would move or disappear only to show up once again in the most unlikely of places.

But after all the experiences, and despite the fact that at the time they may have been frightening and unsettling, Holly and Arden both agree that whatever resided in that home, and probably still resides there today, means no harm.

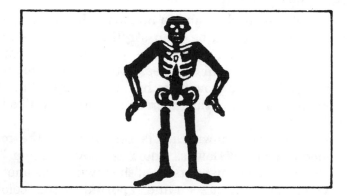

THE MAN IN THE
CELLULOID COLLAR

Not much is known about them, but at least three ghosts have been known to perambulate in and around the quiet town of Bowers Beach.

One, according to Jane Boone, is the mysterious man in the celluloid collar.

On selected nights, and in no particular pattern, this sorrowful figure could be seen strolling along the main street of town. Folks say he was probably very nattily attired in life, but in his restless afterlife, just about all that is visible is the glow from his stiff, shiny collar that glistens in the light of the moon as he silently walks into eternity.

Another well-known tale is set on what the more seasoned citizens of Bowers know as "Lover's Lane."

Along this road just outside of the town walks another anonymous spirit first seen and reported by the "colored people" who gathered at the oyster factory along the river when the high tide came in.

Nobody's really certain what or who the folks were seeing, but supposedly that same ghost that struck fear in the hearts of the blacks back then still haunts that old road. It will be seen on a foggy night along a tight curve deep in the woods. According to some reports, several motorists have claimed to have seen it even up to the time of this writing.

Another ghostly vision has been alleged on the beach near Bowers. It is the spirit of a man who, it is said, once walked into a storm-ravaged bay surf and never came back. Never, at least, as a living, breathing human being! Just south of Bowers Beach is one of the most important and incredible archaeological sites in the country, the Island Field site.

It is one of the oldest documented settlements in the east, and it traces, in graphic terms, a lifestyle which pre-dates written history.

On a windswept, lonely spit of sand on Milford Neck, a roof covers more than 100 exposed graves of an Indian burial ground estimated to be 1,200 years old.

Buried with the skeletons are personal items including trading and bartering items native to distant areas. A comprehensive display and exhibit gallery wraps around the graves, many of which are left in the exact condition they were discovered. The museum is not for the squeamish.

The exhibits and a slide presentation tell the story of the ongoing research being done at Island Field, and knowledgeable staff members are on hand during the season to answer questions.

While there is no official line on the matter, and when asked, workers at Island Field will shy away from discussing in depth, there have always been tales of Indian spirits loose down Milford Neck way.

Ancestors of the Lenni Lenape Indians cherished and utilized the rich land of lower Delaware to the fullest. When white settlers set foot on their property at Lewes Creek in 1631, they were repelled by the Indians.

This first Dutch whaling colony, ill-fated as it may have been, is what opened the door for the determined Europeans to gain a strong foothold in short order and push the Indians deeper inland and rapidly into submission.

As early as 1865, serious archaeological efforts were undertaken to probe the life and times of these lost Native. Americans. Many artifacts were found on the Lewes Shell Heaps on Cape Henlopen in the mid-19th century, but almost exactly 100 years later, in 1965, archaeologists hit "pay dirt" with the Island Field discovery.

There can be only so much space within the professional limitations of Charles Fithian, the curator of archaeology for the Delaware Bureau of Museums. A scientist and researcher by trade, Fithian explained that despite the pragmatic sense of his work and those at Island Field, there is still a strong sense of the mystical and mysterious there.

Fithian recalled the reaction of certain members of the public when the museum around the Indian graves was opened in 1972.

Shortly after the opening, a Delaware Indian princess exorcised the wayward spirits of her ancestors at Island Field. But over the years since then, the archaeologically-acceptable but spiritually-questionable method of displaying the open graves has come under fire from Indian groups and individuals.

There are those who maintain that the exorcism did not "take," and Indian spirits wander in confused states from the Island Field burial ground, around and in Bowers and beyond.

This feeling has spread as far north as Iron Hill, New Castle County, where a fine natural history museum occupies a former one-room school house near an old iron mine.

A spokesman there, keeping science and the supernatural at arm's length, said an Indian skeleton once kept at the museum was returned to Island Field for a proper burial. Somehow, vandals stole the skull, and the burial was carried out without the skull. The museum spokesman said it is possible that the spirit may still be searching for its head somewhere between its grave and Iron Hill.

Iron Hill, incidentally, while as far as a New Castle County site can be from the shore of the bay, has its own ghost legend.

The only battle of the Revolutionary War to be fought in Delaware took place at Cooch's Bridge, just east of Iron

Hill. The hill itself had been the campsite of both British and American troops throughout the conflict, and it is in that time period that the legend of the phantom horseman took root.

Once, there was a small band of colonists camped at Iron Hill. It was lonely duty, and the young men positioned there were raw recruits, fresh out of the back woods and farms of the colonial heartland.

One quiet evening, just after dark, a lone sentry positioned himself on a rock to guard against any intruders into the camp. At once, the young man heard, echoing through the dale below, the thumping of horses' hooves. They drew louder and louder, but through the trees the sentry could see nothing approaching.

Suddenly, as if out of nowhere, a white-robed figure riding atop a milky stallion charged by the lad. Startled, the guard fell from his rocky perch and watched as the pale rider faded into the forest.

Visibly shaken by what he had believed was an encounter with a ghost, the young soldier asked to be relieved of his duty. His superiors noted his obvious fear, and granted his request.

Sure enough, however, his relief was also tormented by the ghostly horseman the very next night. Aware of the possibility that the phantom may pass, the second guard was ready for it. As the figure stormed past, the sentry aimed his rifle and fired. He was certain his aim was true, but all he heard was an evil cackling coming from the rider's sinister mouth.

Again and again the phantom eluded guard after guard at the little camp. Finally, a more seasoned soldier took the midnight watch and stood determined to bring down the "ghost."

About midnight, the horses' hooves thundered from the distance, and the white figure emerged from the darkness. The soldier gripped the trigger of his musket, aimed and blasted away at the form.

There was silence. The horse, minus its rider, leaped

over rocks and fences and made its way into the forest. On the ground near the brave colonist was a lifeless, white-enrobed corpse.

Gingerly, the shooter approached the recipient of his well-placed bullet. He saw immediately that it was nothing more than a British horseman, dressed in a white sheet. He was only a man, playing on the naivete of the young sentries, and not a ghost at all!

THE ETERNAL ROCKER AND
THE VOICE FROM THE GRAVE

It seems fitting somehow that in the process of speaking with dozens of people, spending hundreds of hours in libraries, historical sites and societies, and hundreds more hours "beating the bushes" and beaches of Delaware in search of the supernatural, the most poignant and sobering portrait of the quest was elaborately framed by a man of the cloth.

Rev. Hugh Miller is retired, but as with so many other "retirees," the gentle man in the little house at Slaughter Beach is almost more active than ever.

A former U.S. Navy chaplain and pastor in Morris County, New Jersey, for 35 years, Rev. Miller married a native of Sussex County and settled into retirement in Slaughter Beach in 1980.

He has taken the history of the village under his wing, and is well versed on its limited lore.

It is always disconcerting for a "ghost hunter" to discuss ghostly matters with members of the clergy. But in Rev. Miller's case, the subject was easily approached.

"The whole idea of ghosts," he said, "the spiritual life and all, well something is happening. It is something that people aren't always able to interpret. Some folks interpret it religiously.

"I think your whole outlook on this is not whether it's true or not, but whether somebody **thinks** it's true. That is, I think, a very interesting and healthy outlook.

"You see something, and you're sure you see it. Just because I can't see it doesn't mean it's not there."

Whew! Did that stated philosophy ever make the next question easier to ask! "Reverend," we queried, "do you know any ghost stories?"

He certainly did, and the spook in question wasn't very far away at all.

"There was an old guy who used to live in a house just south of the old store here in Slaughter Beach," Rev. Miller began.

"He lived there in one room, and he would always rock on the porch and wave to people and all. After he died, his kids say that his rocking chair still used to rock.

"That chair remained out on the porch for quite a while, and even though the house was torn down in 1988, those kids won't go by there at night. They believe the old man's ghost is still there."

Rev. Miller's granddaughter, Rachel, added yet another story from the Slaughter Beach area. She talked of a distraught resident of the town who lost his entire family to the ravages of a hurricane many years ago.

It is said that he wandered into the marshes just outside of town, around the Slaughter Neck Ditch. There, the man shot himself.

His ghost supposedly haunts the marshes to this day, and more than one innocent hunter or hiker has had an encounter with his malevolent ghost.

The marsh land on Slaughter Neck is part of the Prime Hook National Wildlife Refuge, which stretches from below Broadkill Beach to Slaughter Beach. From within a section of that nature compound comes yet another story of a restless wraith that walks aimlessly along a trail near the road which leads into Broadkill Beach.

The story is told by a Wilmington man who, because of his prominent standing in the city's banking community, wishes to remain anonymous. Let us call him Ted.

Ted never, ever believed in ghosts. "Not one bit," he said with a strong assertion. "I really can't think of anything that was farther removed from my mind. Even in scouts, when somebody told ghost stories around a camp-fire or whatever, I shrugged it off. I thought it was all a bunch of bunk."

Something happened to Ted one morning at Prime Hook that changed his attitude about ghosts forever.

As one enters Prime Hook, a marvelous pathway called the Boardwalk Trail unfolds into the marshlands. Along the way is the bounty of this preserved portion of Delaware Bay shoreline which is one of 435 sites within the aegis of the National Wildlife Refuge System.

Not far into the Boardwalk Trail, beyond a natural corridor of multiflora rose and up a slight grade, is all that remains of the Jonathan J. Morris farmstead.

Demolished in 1968, the farm house stood for more than two centuries. A brick-and-beam, shingled structure with two substantial chimneys, the place had deteriorated beyond repair. State and local historical authorities picked the building clean of any salvageable features, but the house was leveled.

In it, human drama and human dreams played out for several generations. People laughed, cried, were born and died inside the Morris home, and all that is left is the memory of those emotions and, perhaps, the faint echoes of the souls who occupied the farm and may remain there still.

Ted, old doubting Ted, now believes there is something to all of this "ghost stuff."

"I got to the refuge early one morning in late September," Ted continued. "I sort of make the rounds of all the refuges and parks in the state. I'm not a nature nut or anything, and can't tell a hawk from a hummingbird, but I like to get away from my job and city life and wander through marshes, woods and whatever.

"So there I was. I parked my car in the little lot and went over toward the trail. I had been there a few times before, and pretty well knew my way around.

"This is going to sound strange, but as I walked over past the old cemetery off to the left of the trail, I felt

71

compelled to walk up to it. I always bypassed it the other times I was down there. I didn't give it much thought at all until that morning. I can't explain it, but it just felt as if something was drawing me toward that cemetery."

Ted paused, lit up another cigarette, and settled back into his chair. "I hope nobody I know figures out who I am. If they knew it was me telling you this story, they'd howl! But anyway, I know it happened, and I know it changed my mind about a lot of things.

"Anyway, I walked up toward the cemetery. At first, like I said, it was just a feeling. I can't explain it at all. But as I got closer to the fence that surrounds the cemetery, the sensation got stronger. It seemed focused, if you know what I mean. I was drawn to one particular tombstone."

Ted reflected on the mood of the day. "Maybe it was the surroundings that made it even stranger. The snaggled tree limbs, the eerie rows of corn and the constant cackle of the geese. I must admit that it was a little scary, even for somebody like me who never was too impressed with spook stories.

"I walked almost directly to that one tombstone. It was John Morris's grave. Now, I never heard of this guy, and knew from nothing about the family or even that there was ever a house there. But all of a sudden, as I stood there looking down on the tombstone, I felt an icy sensation, as if my entire body was quickly encased in ice. I shook and shuddered and in a split second tried to fight off whatever it was. I guess I managed to shake it, because it was over very quickly.

"Then, I heard something. It was as if someone was speaking to me from just a few feet away. I don't believe I'm saying this, but it sounded as if someone was speaking from within the graveyard. Of course, nobody was there.

"It wasn't like someone was hiding in the underbrush, whispering my way. No way. What I heard was most definitely coming from inside the railings of the cemetery."

Ted's nerves were obviously shaken by the experience. But his recollection was still not complete. Something would happen that would test Ted's very sanity. "No kidding, I thought I was going nuts. I knew it was not a trick. Nobody could have caused that cold feeling, and nobody could make the sound that was coming from the graveyard.

"It started like a throaty whisper, with nothing particularly understandable. But then, I could understand something. It was a soft, sad young voice simply asking a series of one-word questions. It said 'how?...' and then 'why?...' "

The questions continued for several seconds, perhaps a full minute, according to Ted. "Of course, in that kind of situation, that one minute starts to feel like an hour. But one by one, the words came. 'Who?...,' 'what?...,' and then it repeated itself.

"I was too riveted to the time and place to try to figure out much about it. I remember, at least I think I do, that it was a young voice, and I believe it was a young woman or girl. But do you know what? It seemed to be coming from — and here I go again, I can't believe I'm telling you this — but it seemed to be coming from that one grave, the grave of John Morris."

Ted crushed a cigarette butt into an ashtray and reached immediately for another. As he caught the writer glancing a disparaging look his way, he pointed out that he was not usually a chain smoker, "but whenever I remember that morning, I get a little nervous, I guess."

Ted recalled that there was a stiff wind blowing through the nearby trees, and swift-moving clouds low in the sky added to the mood of the morning. "I just stood there," he continued, "and I wondered if I was going nuts, or if it was really some kind of trick, or what. But the voice was clear and distinct, and although I'll never be able to explain it rationally, it will live with me forever."

After a while, the ghostly voice from the grave seemed to fade, Ted recalled, "I just stood there, and I remember that I gazed toward the clouds. Like I said, I'm not — or at

73

least I wasn't — a believer in this kind of thing, and I'm not terribly religious, but my first thought was that this may have been some kind of message or sign from the great beyond. Who knows?

"I took a deep breath, stood there and thought about what had happened, and went back onto the trail for my walk. Lord knows, I had a lot to think about on that walk!"

Ted has been back to Prime Hook several times since that incident. "Every time," he concluded, "I walk over to John Morris's tombstone and stare down at it for a minute or two. Someday, I'd like to find out more about that family, and maybe I'll have some answers about that girl's voice, and whatever it might all mean. Then again, maybe I don't want to know!"

FIDDLER'S BRIDGE

It is the classic Delaware ghost story. Although the times have most certainly changed since it was first spun so very long ago, the yarn endures.

As the times have changed, so has the locale. Once upon a time, as they say, a sometimes-dusty, sometimes-muddy little road descended from Wilmington. Just south of what is now the St. Georges Bridge, a rickety wooden span carried horses and buggies over Scott Run.

That old road has been replaced by the Du Pont Highway, and that divided four-lane now whisks over Scott Run as if the little stream didn't even exist.

Parker Crossland, who was 92 at the time of this writing, remembers the last of the ox-cart days when roads were more like ditches than pavements. Crossland was interviewed in his tidy farm near the C & D Canal, and despite his age, his wits and wisdom were clear and vivid.

He remembered well when the road over Scott Run was dirt, when a narrow bridge humped over the stream, and the roadway eventually led to an oyster-shell paved causeway lined with willow trees and then into Wilmington.

While today, traffic breezes (all conditions considered) into the city from St. Georges, back then it was a tortuous ride. "I was a grown man until I seen Philadelphia," Crossland recalled.

He also recalled with ease the stories told to him back

then about the ghost that could be conjured up fairly easily down along Scott Run.

"Fiddler's Bridge, they called it," he said. "Back in horse and buggy days, it was a little, wooden bridge and didn't amount to much.

"There used to be sunfish and perch in that old creek. We'd go down there with a string and a pin and catch them. I remember when they used to herd cattle on that road and up over that bridge. That was quite a sight.

"And yeah, they used to tell us kids that if you'd pitch a dime in there, a fiddler would play. I don't know where they got that, though."

Well, Mr. Crossland, it's an old, old story, and while its basic structure and motif are familiar folklore fodder, it is still fascinating to ponder.

Fascinating, yes, but difficult to ponder if one were to venture back to the scene of the haunting. Marginal farmland surrounds the wooded swath of Scott Run, and the roar of traffic on Route 301 is incessant.

But it wasn't like that when the old black man sat, propped up on one of the fence rails of the bridge, and fiddled away from morning to night.

They say he was born to slave parents who had only recently come over from Africa. Some attribute the black family to land owners named Osborn, whose property straddled Scott Run.

The little boy came to be known as Jacob, and from early childhood he was filled with rhythm, music, and the desire to play, dance and sing to anyone who would watch and listen — and some who cared not to.

He fashioned a fiddle with a box and tree branches, and later put that crude instrument aside when an unknown benefactor presented him with a real violin.

Amusing and entertaining to some people, Jacob became an irritant to the caretaker of the farm.

Legend has it that the caretaker became enraged with Jacob and his merrimaking. He pulled him aside, lashed him until he was rendered unconscious, and assumed that the whipping would put an end to his fiddling.

For a while, it did. Jacob was incoherent. Perhaps the whipping had damaged his ability to reason, speak and think. It did not, however, hurt his ability to fiddle.

And fiddle he did. The wild, interminable music led to poor Jacob being banished from his own family.

He found a pleasant spot in the swampy maple and willow woods along Scott Run and built a crude hut. There, by the little bridge, Jacob serenaded the beasts of the forest with his mad music.

Passers-by would hear the fiddling and sometimes they would hand old Jacob a coin for his serenade. He'd pause just long enough to tip his hat, and then return bow to strings.

Was Jacob beaten to insanity by his overseer? Had he become possessed by a demon that drove him into his fiddling frenzy?

Nobody can ever say. But it is said that one night, perhaps in a fit or seizure, or by sheer accident, Jacob fell into the shallow water of the creek and drowned.

The fiddling was silenced.

They pulled Jacob's lifeless body from the water, and all who knew him or knew of his bridge-side fiddling knew at once they would never hear his music ever again.

Or would they?

Not long after Jacob was laid to rest, stories of the fiddlin' apparition on the bridge over Scott Run began to circulate.

A band of taverned-out lads, crossing over the bridge late one night, joked as their steeds clip-clopped over the rustic span.

They had remembered passing by many times before and tossing a coin Jacob's way for the nod of the head, tip of the hat and slash of the bow they would receive in return.

One of the men quipped to the other, "Let's throw a coin in the creek — maybe old Jacob's ghost will play us a tune!"

The men all laughed uproariously at such a notion. One of them took a coin from his pocket, and amid the mocking of his pals, hurled it into the stream.

At once, rising above the sounds of the swamp and cutting through the darkness, was the eerie sound of fiddling. Emerging from the water was a whitish glow. The men pulled back on the reins and were frozen in their places.

The milky figure seemed to take shape and then fade as the fiddling music rose and fell in intensity.

Within a few minutes, the sounds of frogs and owls returned to command the night. The fiddling faded and the phantom retreated to the waters from whence it came.

The men remained motionless for several moments before they glanced at one another. Their eyes were as wide and white as the moon that floated in the steel sky over the swamp maples.

Slowly and tentatively, one of the men pulled his pocket watch out and nervously told his companions, "W-w-well, fellows, looks like it's midnight. We'd best get goin' home!"

Suddenly silent, the men slapped their horses and headed home. It was a night they would never forget.

And to this very day, the ghost of Jacob, the fiddler, awaits only the toss of a coin into the creek at the site of the old bridge.

Do that, they say, under a bright moon at midnight and prepare yourself for the sweetest fiddle music you have ever heard.

TALES OF VOODOO,
MURDER AND MAGIC

The proud and yet mysterious heritage of the black population of the Delaware coastal region has added rather unique touches to the folklore of the area.

Twice and thrice-told tales speak of chaps such as Arnsy Maull, who was sometimes called the "wizard of Belltown."

In this black enclave near Lewes, Arnsy lived alone in a simple home by the marsh. He was well equipped with potions, notions and concoctions designed as aids in his wizardry.

It was said Arnsy could conjure up ghosts and cure any and all ills of the living. He was often put to the test by those who knew of his skills, and it is reported that when he died, a fierce storm lashed Belltown. It was an enraged Satan, trying unsuccessfully to snatch Arnsy's soul from its eventual destination.

Even more deeply seated in the history and lore of certain areas of Delaware are the enigmatic folks known over the years as "Moors."

Just what are the "Moors of Cheswold," as they are sometimes called?

Characterized as strikingly handsome people with features of both negro and caucasian, this small society has, over the years, settled mostly in Cheswold, just north of Dover and in the Indian River area of Sussex County.

The "free Moors" is how a 1790 document referred to what was once a very clear and distinct sub-society.

So distinct were these "Moors" that well into the latter half of the twentieth century, the state of Delaware still reserved "Moor" as a designation of ethnicity — although nobody has been quite sure exactly what a "Moor" really was.

At about the point where Indian River widens into the bay, near Oak Orchard and Riverdale, was the highest concentration of Moors in southern Delaware.

It was once called "Down Sockum" by the locals because of the widespread Sockum family.

With their mixed racial features, the Moors were more often considered "free Negroes" by whites. In the first half of the nineteenth century, with tension between whites and blacks running high in Delaware, the racial definition of Moors became an issue in a trial.

A white man with an apparent vendetta against a "Moor" named Levin Sockum, had Sockum arrested for allegedly selling a gun to a "free mulatto" named Isaac Harmon.

The issue of black-white-mulatto-Moor surfaced in the 1855 trial in the Sussex County Courthouse, and it was an 80-year-old Nanticoke Indian who had anglicized her name to Lydia Clark who provided damning testimony.

Clark related the story which had been handed down to her from her parents and grandparents. As she told it, both Sockum and Harmon, despite their strong Caucasian features and their tan skin, were descendents of the "Moors," which had very clear Negro origins.

Sockum was fined twenty dollars for the illegal sale of the gun and ammunition to Harmon, since both were just "Negro" enough to be under certain restrictions as set down by prevailing laws.

Until 1921, Moors in the Indian River Hundred of Sussex County had their own segregated school. They shared it for a time with children of Nanticoke Indians, until integration of all such schools was mandated by federal law.

The association of the Nanticokes and Moors is strong. Among the many theories about the origin of the tan-skinned, handsome people is that they trace their beginnings on these shores to a mid-eighteenth century wreck of Moroccan sailors near the present Cape Henlopen.

The sailors were given aid and comfort by the Nanticokes, and over the years they inter-married and their offspring have had the characteristics now attributed to the "Moors."

Another similar theory unites the same two parties, but claims the Moroccans landed intentionally on the Delaware coast to start a colony.

Yet another story traces the entire colony to one woman and one man. But, as folklore is wont to do, the story splinters into many shards.

Take, for example, one version which mentions a Congo chief who was brought here as a slave. It is said his name was Chief Requa, and he eventually won the heart of a female, white landowner.

She bore him several children, they intermingled with the Nanticokes and the misnomered "Moors" were born.

Then, there's the variation of that which alleges that Requa was a woman. She was, in fact, a wealthy Spanish woman who lived near Lewes. She chose as her lover a slave who was either of Congolese or Moroccan descent. Whatever, she bore him many children, and . . . well, you know the rest.

Some say the many lovely lotus lilies that grow along the Saint Jones River near Cheswold came from seeds from yet another entry in the divergent theories about the Moors.

A narrowly-held proposition has the original "Moors" coming to what is now Delaware on a crude craft from Egypt. In that vessel, which was supposedly unearthed several years ago in an archaeological dig, were the lotus seeds and the progenitors of what were to become known, quite mistakingly if this tale is to be believed, as "Moors."

Blacks play another role in an enduring legend of southern Delaware. It is the tale of the evil Patty Cannon. A powerfully-built woman who lived on a farm near the Delaware-Maryland border town now known as Reliance, Patty Cannon used that border as a wedge for her alleged evil-doings.

The wife of Jesse Cannon, who in 1821 was sentenced to 39 lashes of the whip on the public pillory and to have "the soft part of each ear cut off" as his punishment for kidnapping slaves, Patty Cannon supposedly continued Jesse's slave trading after his death.

Slave trading was illegal in Delaware, but not in Maryland. So, Patty Cannon would carry out her misdeeds in Delaware and flee to Maryland when the heat was applied.

It has been stated that Patty Cannon, with the help of other slave dealers in the area, kidnapped blacks who were attempting to escape within and just outside the "tracks" of the Underground Railroad. They were held captive at a tavern where rich southern plantation owners and slavers would rendezvous with the kidnappers.

More often than not, however, these wealthy dealers in human flesh became victims of Patty Cannon's wrath.

In 1829, Sussex County officials began to follow leads which led to the shallow graves of several slave dealers, slaves and children who had been murdered by the vicious Mrs. Cannon.

In April, 1829, she was arrested for four counts of murder and held for trial.

In the interim, Patty Cannon confessed to ten murders, to being an accomplice in twelve more and had two more killings planned.

Before she could come to trial, Patty Cannon further admitted to the murders of not only her husband, but also her own child.

Following these revelations, Patty managed to fashion a lethal dose of poison as she waited in her cell. Her final act of death-dealing was committed on herself.

She was buried near the Sussex County Jail, but her bones were later re-interred at the county "potter's field."

In the transporting of the skeletal remains, a Dover law clerk managed to spirit away her skull.

A morbid curiosity, the skull eventually wound up in the Dover Public Library, where there have been many tales of ghostly occurrences surrounding it, while library spokesmen deny there are any ghosts in the library. The skull, which those in the know say may or may not really be that of Patty Cannon, is kept in a hat box in the library, and may be viewed upon request.

Downstate a bit, in the Reliance area, they say the old Cannon property is haunted by the tormented spirits of the murdered and the murderess.

GHOSTS OF THE RICH, FAMOUS, POOR AND OBSCURE

It is difficult at times to gather stories of ghosts, phantoms and the unexplained. Officials who maintain and care for historical properties are reluctant to talk about the rumors that swirl around those properties, for reasons which have never been quite clear to the authors of this volume.

The phenomenon is not peculiar to Delaware. While an entire community may speak freely of the alleged hauntings of a particular public building or plot, those who are paid out of the public treasury often refuse to broach the subject of ghosts.

Often, they will begin the bureaucratic buck-passing with a raft of telephone contacts which must be made before anyone will offer a "company line" on the matter. Too often, however, the buck never stops anywhere. The ghost hunter is forced to go "underground" for the story.

The strange occurrences at the Dickinson Mansion south of Dover are examples of widely-known stories hushed by those who choose to stifle them for personal or professional reasons.

Up and down the shore of the Delaware Bay, the unexplained incidents at the home of the lawyer, writer and political figure John Dickinson are perfect examples of "they say" ghost stories.

They say that there are tape recordings made in the mansion which quite clearly depict the scratching of a quill pen on parchment, the crumbling of that paper and the tossing of a wad of paper across a room in the rooms once occupied by the man who has been called the "penman of the Revolution."

Volunteers and staff members, "they say," have come into the bed chamber of the house, again when it was certain no one was inside, and have found the master bed unmade by mid-day. "They say" further that Dickinson was known to have taken naps in his day, and "they say" the tousled bed may be evidence that it is Dickinson's spirit which walks the rooms and halls of his former mansion.

It's a split verdict on the reported and reputed ghosts of the lovely historic district of New Castle.

While some of the spirits in the old harbor town have been the subject of articles and mentions in diverse publications, others have fallen through the cracks of credibility.

One of the more prominent phantoms is the one which haunts an old inn at 216 Delaware Street.

Built in 1683, the building was once owned by David Finney, lawyer, soldier and respected Delawarean. It has served most recently as a bed and breakfast.

The fine building has been lovingly restored and expanded by Tom and Louise Hagy, who are generally divided on their beliefs in things that go bump in the night. Louise is perceived as the "believer" while Tom remains the eternal skeptic.

Still, Tom cannot deny the mysterious events which took place before his very eyes. On the overview, it would seem that whatever spirit may wander the suites and hallways of the David Finney Inn might just be challenging Tom Hagy's skepticism.

"When we first bought the building," Tom recalled, "the woman who was selling it to us had a little dog. We went through the building and the dog followed us everywhere. We went up on the second floor, and then up to the third. That dog, who had been no more than two feet from us at all times, absolutely refused to go up on that third floor. It just sat there and kind of whined the whole time we were up there. I thought, well, this was just a weird dog, and left it at that."

Those who study the paranormal and the supernatural claim that young children and animals are often the first to notice a spectral presence, and quite often are the most deeply affected by the spirits.

Tom continued his story. "I had my own dog at the time, a cocker spaniel. We bought the building and began to renovate it. About a month or two later, the same reaction that woman's dog had hit our dog. I thought this was a little nutty. That dog had never let me out of his sight before. I wasn't thinking ghosts, though, I just thought something was strange up there on the third floor."

Hagy said there was yet another incident involving a member of the canine species — or, in this case, members.

"As construction continued, we hired guard dogs — a big Doberman and a big German Shepherd. We put them in the building at night. The guy used to bring them in when we were leaving in the evening and he came to pick them up in the morning. They were mean, vicious dogs. But even **they** wouldn't go up on that third floor!"

Even after these trained attack dogs cowered from whatever power repelled them from the upper floor, Tom Hagy could not pin the episodes on anything ghostly. That attitude might have changed a bit, however, as the months ensued.

"Eventually," he continued, "the building was completed. One time, up on the third floor, something very strange happened. The windows up there are thirty-five, forty feet above the sidewalk in the back. There's no way you can get to them. They're double-hung windows and totally inaccessible. But, they used to come open at night, on their own. We'd come in, knowing they were shut, but they'd be open!

"We'd have guests stay in the room, and they would tell us they'd be in there at night and the windows would suddenly open up at night. Then, I started to think, 'what the hell's going on here?' "

Tom chuckled cautiously. The bizarre happenings continued. He remembered that when he bought the place, "there was an old black fellow who came along with the building. He told us some strange stories, but I just thought he had an odd sense of humor."

Maybe, maybe not.

One Sunday night, when there were no guests booked at the inn, Tom decided to investigate the occurrences.

"I went into the room next to the suite where all the activity had taken place. Before I went to bed in that adjacent room, I took a stick and angled it from the top of the lower sash, diagonally across the top window to the other corner. I did that to both windows. There was absolutely, positively no way those windows could come open.

"I locked the bedroom door and went to bed in the next room. I got up at six o'clock the next morning, went into the other room and those damn sticks were on the bureau and the windows were open!"

Tom's skepticism received a solid punch, and was nearly on the mat.

It may have gone down for the count in more recent times.

"It wasn't long ago (from the time of the research for the book) when we had some guests who suggested we beef up the locks of the guest suites. So, I had latches put on the inside of the doors, so they could lock the doors from inside. They were the kind of latches where you could open the door about four inches to peek out, but that was about it.

"The first thing I know, the damn latch wound up locked inside that room! Inside! There is no way in hell you could lock that latch from the outside . . . no way! What's more, there is no way in hell you could get into that room without a forty foot ladder."

Pow! Tom began to reel from the force of yet another blow to his beliefs.

"Well, I managed to squeeze a hacksaw in and sawed the latch so we could get inside the room. There was, of course, nobody in the room, and nothing was disturbed.

"I replaced the latch, and do you know what? About a month later, the same damned thing happened!"

Tom isn't as quick these days to refute the tales of the haunting of the David Finney Inn. "There have been other reports of people feeling presences in other parts of the building," he admitted, "but I kind of discount that. I cannot, though, discount what actually happened to me up on that third floor because I'm here to say that I saw it!"

There is a recurring story around New Castle that the Amstel House, which was built by David Finney's father, Dr. John Finney, is haunted.

The house, now an historical museum, was also once the home of a Delaware governor, Nicholas Van Dyke.

About a block away from the David Finney Inn, the Amstel House is reported to be connected to the Finney by an underground tunnel which has probably long since been destroyed by street building and utility construction.

Tom Hagy noted that there is architectural evidence in both the Amstel House and the David Finney Inn that there really was a tunnel.

When the ghost story researcher suggested that the alleged hauntings of the Amstel and Finney buildings might be connected by the old tunnel, Hagy chuckles.

A nervous chuckle.

Pow!

The very streets and back alley ways of New Castle may be haunted by the spirits of headless Dutch soldiers. Author Walter A. Powell, in his History of Delaware, wrote of the wandering warriors:

"At certain seasons after nightfall," he wrote, "you may see headless Dutchmen in strange and ghostly attire, marching up and down the shore."

Powell continued, "There are those who have listened to the noise of cannon balls rolling in the dust over floors, which no mortal eye can ever see. And often, when there is a tempest, the booming of guns will be heard above the roar of the storm, and from spectral ships floating upon the bosom of the river will come the wailing voices of women and children who are still sorrowing for their last homes."

Thus, there are those in Delaware who have chosen not to deny the rich folklore of the state but to celebrate it. The ghost stories of this proud state are vivid, indelible anecdotes to the deep history of Delaware.

There are many of these spectral tales, and while this book attempts to focus on those along the shoreline of the ocean and bay, it would be remiss in not mentioning those sagas which are very often nothing more than skeletal foundations of legends and lore.

For example, is there a ghost in the Dover Public Library, as some folks say? Could it be that of confessed murderer Patty Cannon, whose skull is allegedly kept inside the library?

Do ghostly hounds howl at the moon outside the Public Building in Wilmington? Could they be accompanied by the spirit of George Read Riddle, whose home once stood on that site?

Over in Newark, there are tales of hauntings on the Blue and Gold Club, and at the campus theatre and in the Penny Hill House on the Philadelphia Pike.

Noisy spirits have been detected at a home near Quarryville, and a flaming man has been reported on a bridge across Featherbed Run near that same town.

Rockwood, the spectacular Gothic mansion which is now a park and museum, is said to harbor an apparition, as is the Allee House at Bombay Hook.

Two homes on S. Main St. in Camden provide havens for two very divergent ghosts. A cat visible only to children stalks the floors of one structure, while just down the street a sad spirit haunts those who possess the power to detect it.

The ghost is that of a young woman who supposedly died in childbirth in what was her and her husband's dream home way back in the early part of the nineteenth century. The mourning man is said to have played "their song" on the violin almost constantly following his mate's death.

Now, long after his passing, some people still say they can hear the sorrowful tune being played sweetly by an unseen violinist who serenades at the base of the main staircase.

Ghosts have been sensed in a home on Main Street in Middletown, in a building of Wesley College in Dover, and there is hardly a village or town in Delaware which does not have its "haunted house."

Downstate, a benevolent spirit of a former miller still walks the ancient planks of Abbott's Mill near Milford. A church at Selbyville is famous for its breezy wraith, and colorful Tony J. Morgan, who has operated a collectibles/curiosities store in town since moving there from his native South Philadelphia in 1970, swears he can feel somebody (or some thing) watching over him when he ventures upstairs in the 1834-vintage building.

In nearby Dagsboro, at least two homes are infested with spirits and the old house on a chicken farm near Roxana has a ghost that moves artwork on walls and creates a general disturbance in the former strawberry plantation.

Between Georgetown and Milford, just off Route 113, is what some people call the Delaware equivalent of the New Jersey Pine Barrens.

It is Redden State Forest, a patchwork of state land which was once a forest preserve of the Junction and Breakwater Railroad division of the Pennsylvania Railroad. The land, which was used for hunting and the recreational pursuits of Pennsy executives, was improved as a state forest by the Civilian Conservation Corps in the 1930s.

The ranger's house of the state forest was once a railroad station, and it seems that strange things have happened in that home over the years.

Lloyd Simmons, forest manager, said there was a death recorded in the house in the early 1900s, and the odd occurrences in the place have been attributed to the young woman who died there under mysterious circumstances.

"We knew that there was a person who died in here," Simmons said, "so we got to talking about the 'resident ghost.' That seemed to explain all the unexplainable noises we would hear."

Simmons said voices and random sounds would be heard in unoccupied upstairs rooms, and electrical devices would turn on and off with no human aid. "It was all the ghost's fault," quipped Simmons.

Ron Davidson, a New York City native and a law student at the time of this writing, discussed his own recollections of life, or more properly, afterlife, in and around Redden State Forest.

Sitting in the cramped quarters of the Fenwick Island police station, Davidson, who was working that summer as a police officer in the resort town, said he had first-hand knowledge of the spirit inside the old rail station-hunting lodge.

"Several people over the years have heard voices inside that place," he said. "I was dating a girl who lived there, and every time I went in there, I got chills. It was eerie."

Davidson recalled bits and pieces of other legends which have swirled around Redden over the years. He talked of the story of the headless figure which supposedly walks along Route 113 in Ellendale State Forest, just north of Redden. In talking with other police officers from that area, they report what they feel to be an excessive number of traffic accidents along the afflicted stretch. Whether the "haunting" of that road has anything to do with it, nobody will speculate.

Others in the Redden crossroads area have reported vague tales of a pair of spooks which wander the railroad right-of-way just north of Georgetown.

Near Bridgeville, a story persists of the ghost of a money-hoarding old man who used to play tricks on residents as they slept. The ghost eventually ran into a brave mortal who challenged it and demanded to know why he was haunting the house.

The spirit led the man to a pot of gold coins which was buried in the basement of the home. After the man took the treasure in his possession, the ghost was never heard from again.

Back along the shore, there are tales of the ghost of a black man which rises at "The Homestead" in Rehoboth, and strange references to the bedraggled, confused spirit of Eddie Rickenbacker which has been seen on a beach at Bethany.

So, there are ghosts all over Delaware. And, for the most part, Delawareans are eager to share them with one another. Folks such as Kim Burdick, Dave Hugg, William P. Frank, Dorothy Pepper and many more have even gone out of their way to collect and preserve those fascinating tales which help add a bit of mystery to all the history.

When the Delaware Folklore Society was established, it took upon itself the charge of seeing to it that these cultural gems of the state would never be forgotten. Born out of discussions by scholars at the University of Delaware, the Folklore Society came into being on June 5, 1950. Appropriately, it seems, a man named Charles Dickens (no, not **that** . . .) was elected secretary of the society.

In Volume No. 1 of the society's superb Folklore Bulletin, the principles of collecting folklore were presented. And, the mission of the society was outlined: ". . . to preserve songs, sayings and 'supernatural' tales of ghosts, banshees, fairies, healers, omens, dreams, vampires and witches."

Banshees? Witches? Vampires? In Delaware?

Perhaps our ghost-hunting job has only just begun!

We hope you have enjoyed the book. And indeed, while the words now end, the stories never will. A contact address is provided elsewhere in this book. The authors and publishers welcome any and all comments, and especially any ghost story which might have eluded the authors in the course of their research. Many, many, certainly must have.

ACKNOWLEDGEMENTS

The publication of this book would not have been possible without the cooperation of many individuals, the services of many institutions and the resources of many publications.

The authors extend their sincere appreciation to the following people who have been of great help during the research and writing of "Ghost Stories of the Delaware Coast":

Hazel Brittingham, Dorothy Pepper, Kim Burdick, Barbara Gallas, Michael Kennedy, park interpreter and Eric Pearson, volunteer, both at Cape Henlopen State Park; Rachel Miller, Bill Beauchamp, of Anglers Motel, Lewes; Charles Fithian, curator of archaeology, Delaware Bureau of Museums and History; Arden Nagy, Joan Nagy, Margaret Dunham, Rev. Hugh Miller, Gene and Suzanne Racz, at Mispillion Lighthouse Marina; Nancy Kemble, Mary Perez, Gregory King, Henry Marshall, David Burdash, director, and Freda J. Campbell, public relations director, both of the Wilmington Library; Ron Davidson, Tony J. Morgan, Tom Hagy, Lori Rader, of the Wilmington Library; Barbara Benson and Ellen Peterson, both of the Historical Society of Delaware; Susan Ledger, of the Rehoboth Beach Library; Lloyd Simmons, manager of Redden State Forest; Holly Downs, Jane Boone, Cordelia Daisey, Frances Gravette, Max Yela, of the special collections department of the University of Delaware Library . . .

. . . and many others whose names were never given or recorded. We thank you all for your help and for keeping the heritage and folklore of Delaware intact for generations to savor.

SELECTED BIBLIOGRAPHY

Books:

Bassett, Fletcher S., "Legends and Superstitions of the Sea and of Sailors," Singing Tree Press, Detroit, 1971.

Bevan, Wilson Lloyd, "History of Delaware, Past and Present," Lewes Historical Publishing Co., New York City, 1929.

Burdick, Kim, "Once of a Night: Ghost Stories Told in Delaware," 1986.

Cullen, Virginia, "History of Lewes, Delaware," Daughters of the American Revolution, 1956.

Delaware State Planning Office, "History, Historic Sites and Buildings of Lewes, Delaware," 1969.

Federal Writers Project, "Delaware: A Guide to the First State," Hastings House, New York City.

Frank, William P., "Stories and Legends of the Delaware Capes."

Glennon, T. J., "Backroads, U.S.A.," Collier Books, New York City, 1988.

Jagendorf, Moritz Adolf, "Upstate, Downstate: Folk Stories of the Middle Atlantic States," The Vanguard Press, New York City, 1949.

Marvil, James E., "Pilots of the Bay and River Delaware," Sussex Press, 1965.

Myers, Arthur, "The Ghostly Register," Contemporary Books, Chicago and New York City.

Pepper, Dorothy Williams, "Folklore of Sussex County, Delaware," Sussex County Bicentennial Committee, 1976.

Powell, Walter A., "History of Delaware," Christopher Publishing House, Boston, 1928.

Scharf, J. Thomas, "History of Delaware," Philadelphia, 1888.

Snow, Edward Rowe, "Ghosts, Gales and Gold," Dodd, Mead and Co., New York City.

Spencer, John Wallace, "Limbo of the Lost Today," Phillips Publishing Co.

Voynick, Stephen M., "The Mid-Atlantic Treasure Coast," Middle Atlantic Press, Wallingford, Pa., 1984.

Walls, Bruce, "Tales of Old Dover," 1977.

Newspapers, Magazines, Assorted Sources:
Wilmington Evening Journal, Wilmington Morning News, Delaware Coast Press, The Whale, Peninsula Pacemaker, Delaware Today, Delaware Folklore Bulletin, The Beachcomber, University of Delaware Publications, Lewes Chamber of Commerce.

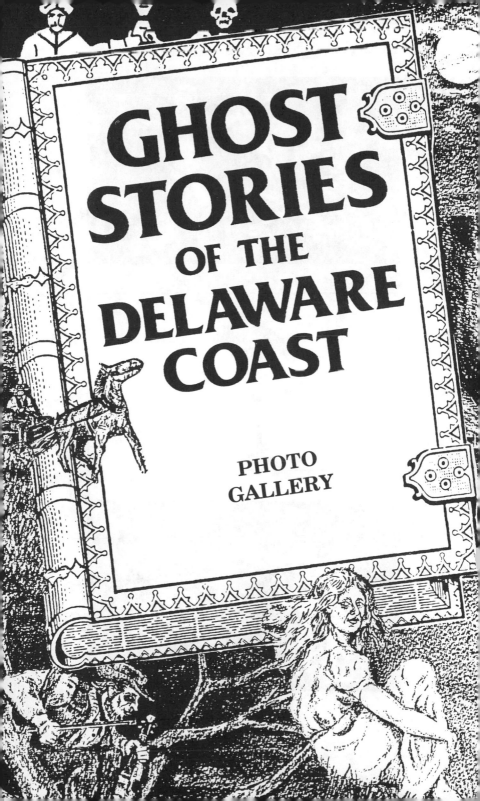

GHOST STORIES

OF THE

DELAWARE COAST

PHOTO
GALLERY

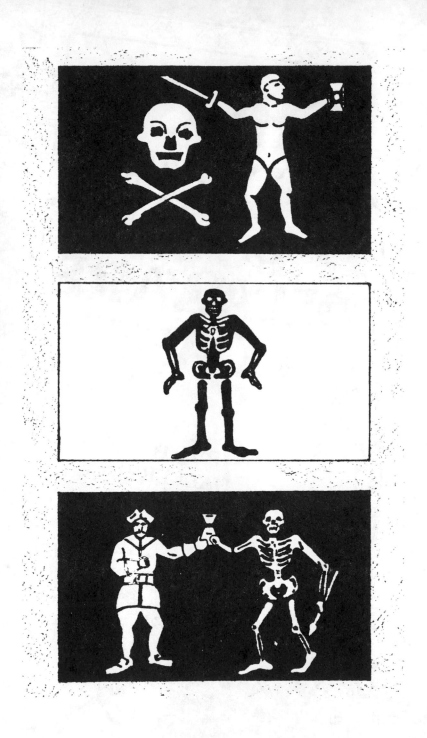

Do ghosts walk the ancient floors of the Cannonball House in Lewes?
Some have had unexplainable experiences in the historic structure.

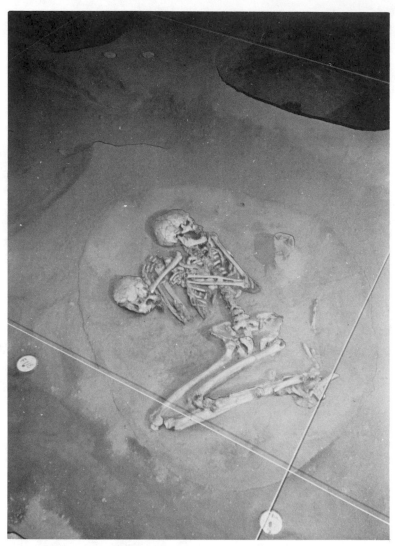

Several legends have evolved from the archaeological work done at the Island Field site near Milford, where several Indian graves were discovered.

A strange encounter greeted one man at the Morris family cemetery at Prime Hook.

It was along this stretch of road where a ghostly fiddler once frightened Sussex Countians.

The Great Cypress Swamp in Lower Delaware is a foreboding place.

Legends of swamp creatures and spirits have long been a part of life
near the cypress swamp known as Burnt Swamp.

Even in broad daylight, the roadway through Burnt Swamp is eerie.

Several ghosts are said to inhabit the Addy-Sea in Bethany Beach.

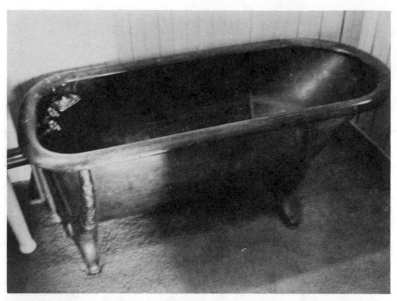

This old copper bath tub has been known to vibrate violently, and the action is linked to a ghost in the Addy-Sea Bed and Breakfast.

A ghostly form has been seen by the bed in this room at the Addy-Sea.

Witnesses report seeing an apparition on this bed at the Addy-Sea in
Bethany Beach.

Co-author David J. Seibold peers out a window in one of the haunted rooms of the Addy-Sea.

Does the ghost of a pirate walk the docks of the marina in Lewes?

The ghosts of Dutch soldiers have been seen by the ragged remains of old docks in New Castle.

Located amid fertile Sussex County farmland, old Fort Saulsbury may still imprison the spirits of soldiers who have passed through the giant bunkers.

Those who enter Fort Saulsbury cannot help but feel a strange sensation.

Chain-rattling ghosts wander the ramparts, rooms and parade ground of Fort Delaware.

Ghostly visions have been seen on stretches of the Delaware, ocean and bay shores.

This is Sam, who occasionally masquerades as the horned "Henlopen Devil."

ABOUT THE AUTHORS

David J. Seibold, an avid fisherman and scuba diver, maintains residences in Reading, Pa. and Barnegat Light, N.J..

A graduate of Penn State University, Seibold is a member of the Barnegat Light Scuba and Rescue Team and operates his own charter boat, the Sea-Bold, out of Barnegat Light.

He is a former commodore of the Rajah Temple Yacht Club and is a decorated Vietnam Campaign veteran.

Seibold is also employed as an account executive at WEEU Broadcasting Co. in Reading, Pa. He is a member of many civic and social organizations.

Charles J. Adams III has written numerous articles, songs and stories, and has authored three books on ghost stories in his native Pennsylvania as well as six books on ghosts and shipwrecks with Seibold.

He is a morning radio personality at WEEU radio in Reading and is the Reading Eagle newspaper's chief travel correspondent.

Adams is a past president of the Reading Public Library and also sits on the executive council and editorial board of the Historical Society of Berks County. He is also a member of the board of directors of the Penn State Alumni Society of the Berks Campus, the Berks County Visitors Information Association, and the Berks County Chapter, American Heart Association.

ABOUT THE ARTIST

J. M. Sponge Washburn is a graduate of Birming-
ham-Southern College and Pratt Institute. A native Ten-
nesseean, he now resides in Trenton and Barnegat Light,
N.J.

Washburn, whose work is exhibited nationally, is a
full-time artist and instructor of art at New York University.

An avid sport fisherman, his concern for the preservation of the ocean and wildlife is reflected in his prints and
paintings.